American Luchadore

by

Mark Muncy

SOMETHING DIFFERENT

Published by Dark House Publications

All rights retained by author

Mark Muncy

510 49th Avenue North, St. Petersburg, FL 33703, U.S.A.

First printing, March 2008

Copyright© Mark Muncy, 2007

Printed in the United States of America

PUBLISHER'S NOTE

This is a work of fiction. Names, characters, places and incidents either are the product of the author's imagination or are used fictionally or in parody. Any resemblance to actual persons living, dead or undead, business establishments, events, or locales is entirely coincidental.

ISBN 978-0-6151-95841

51295

This screenplay is for Amanda, Beth, Callie and Mom. You are the ladies in my life that mean more to me then all the treasures of the world.

Special thanks to the following people:

Rich Tucholka, for allowing me to throw in Bureau 13.

Nick Pollota, for helping me discover the joy of writing.

Jim Butcher, for showing me that magic is possible.

Scott Kurtz, for making me smile and a helpful push.

El Santo, for showing me the world according to Lucha.

Derrick Fish for the wonderful cover illustrations.

All the comic artists who contributed to this wonderful idea.

La Flower, for letting me talk to El Hijo Del Santo.

Lloyd Kaufman, that told me "more breasts, more blood, smaller budget."

A quick note about this edition:

In 2006 I finished the following screenplay, my first. I submitted it and got generally high marks at various screenwriting contests but every one stated it would never work as a film. I tried retooling it for a comic book, but it just didn't work. I've since re-written it and have it to a nice filmable script that may actually see the light of day. For those of us who dream big, however, I present you the untold real story of Rey Supremo.

-Mark Muncy 2007

FADE IN

BEGIN DREAM SEQUENCE

EXT. ALLEY -- NIGHT

CARLOTTA runs through the alley being chased by some unseen
assailant. Carlotta is a young lady but a striking beauty.
She is currently scared to death. She runs to the end of
the alley and realizes she is trapped, boxed in on all
sides.

                    CARLOTTA
          No! Get away! I don't have any money!

A MASKED THUG stalks toward her as Carlotta tries to press
herself back against the wall.

At the front of the alley RAY pulls up in a shiny
convertible. This is Ray as he dreams himself to be. He
wears a shiny suit and his ever present Luchadore mask. He
is athletic but stocky and built for action. He has an
irreverent wit and a masterful skill at sarcasm.

                    RAY
          Hey! Tall dark and gruesome, that's no
          way to treat a lady!

Ray leaps from the car and grabs the masked thug. He
wrestles him to the ground. They quickly regain their feet
and begin to circle each other in a classic wrestling
stand-off. Ray pounces on the thug and pins him to he
ground. He pulls the mask off the thug to reveal that he
is really a were-wolf. This were-wolf is very 60's B-movie
level. He has a hairy face and hairy clawed hands.

Ray is shocked to see this but it quickly turns into a
smile. Ray quickly wrenches a pipe loose from the wall of
the alley and swings it at the were-wolf. He circles
around to Carlotta and catches the flash of silver from her
necklace.

                    RAY (CONT'D)
          Pardon me, fair lady. I find myself in
          need of your necklace.

                    CARLOTTA
          If you think it will help.

Carlotta slips off her necklace and quickly tosses it to
Ray. He ties it around the end of the pipe and slams it
against the were-wolf knocking him back to a wall of the
alley. Then Ray plunges the silver tipped pipe into the
were-wolf's chest.

Ray walks over to the fallen body of the were-wolf who is
slowly turning human again. He crouches over the body.

                    RAY
          Sleep well, valiant foe. Your soul is
          now at peace.

After closing the eyes of the fallen were-wolf, he stands
and walks over to Carlotta. He hands her back her necklace
after cleaning it in a handkerchief. She smiles, then
swoons into his arms.

                    CARLOTTA
          How can I ever repay you?

                    RAY
          I was only doing my duty as a
          luchadore. Protecting innocents and
          rescuing damsels in distress.

                    CARLOTTA
          I think I know a way.

Carlotta stands and kisses Ray through his mask. She
starts to pull his mask up. Ray stops her.

                    RAY
          No. I must never remove my mask in
          public. I would lose my honor and my
          power as a luchadore.

                    CARLOTTA
          Is there anything else I can remove
          then?

Carlotta pulls him close and kisses him again. She kisses
down his neck. She pulls back from his embrace and her
eyes widen. Her mouth opens to reveal huge fangs. Ray
struggles to pull away, but she is too strong. Her fangs
plunge into his neck.

END DREAM SEQUENCE

INT. RAY'S APARTMENT -- MORNING

Ray's Apartment is a typical efficiency. It is one large
room with a couch that is currently folded out into a bed
taking up a large portion of the room. There is a small
kitchen area with a microwave, fridge, stove and sink.
There is a small TV with a collection of Luchadore movies
next to it. On the wall behind the fold out couch is a
poster of an El Santo movie. There is a small workout
bench in one corner of the room. Ray is wearing a T-shirt
and boxers and his ever-present mask. Ray sits bolt
upright in bed. He is visibly shaken by his dream.

                    RAY
          That's it. I am never having chili-
          dogs before bed again.

Ray staggers out of bed and heads to the bathroom, as he
begins his day.

INT. RAY'S BATHROOM -- MORNING

The shower is running and we see Ray's mask hanging on the
towel hook. He reaches for a towel, but we can't see his
face due to the mirror being clouded with steam. He dries
his hair with the towel and puts on his mask. Then he
wipes off the mirror. We never see his unmasked face.

EXT. CITY STREET -- DAY

Ray steps out of his apartment building. It is a small
building, and not in the best part of town. The street is
cluttered and has the occasional rundown car parked along
it. Ray looks up at the sun, then puts his hands in his
pockets and heads out. He is wearing another T-shirt and
jeans.

EXT. BAR -- DAY

Ray walks into a bar that has a sign out front that says
"NOW HIRING BOUNCERS".

                    BAR MANAGER (O.S.)
          Did Justin put you up to this? Is this
          some kind of joke? You don't even have
          a driver's license?

Ray walks back out of the bar. Head down.

EXT. RESTAURANT -- DAY

Ray heads into a restaurant which has a sign that says,
"NOW HIRING DISH"

                         RESTAURANT MANAGER (O.S.)
                What's with the mask? Were you burned
                by acid or something? You're not some
                illegal alien or anything?

Ray heads out of the restaurant and has the same slump as
before.

EXT. CONVENIENCE STORE -- DAY

Ray walks into a convenience store that has a sign that
says "NOW HIRING, NO EXPERIENCE NECESSARY!" He figures
they might just be desperate enough to hire him.

There is the sound of a shotgun blast. Ray quickly runs
out of the store. A CONVENIENCE STORE MANAGER is standing
in the doorway with a shotgun, as Ray runs out of shot.

EXT. RECREATION CENTER PLAYGROUND -- DAY

Ray is teaching a group of KIDS (Aged 8-11) some basic
wrestling. He seems truly happy here and the kids are
enjoying themselves. He is currently showing them some
basic moves. SALLY the recreation center manager motions
for Ray to come over to her. Ray hands his coaches whistle
to a younger assistant and heads over to Sally.

                         SALLY
                Ray, you've done wonders with those
                kids.

                         RAY
                I'm not so sure. They were pretty
                rough and tumble before I got a hold of
                them. I'm just teaching them some
                basic wrestling moves to help them
                learn some self defense.

                         SALLY
                They are much better off now, than they
                have been in years. Those kids didn't
                have much of anything. We were just
                some place that they had less chance of

getting into drugs. Their parents want
the best for them. They just can't
afford much.

                    RAY
Well, I'm just happy to do my part.

                    SALLY
Summer isn't going to last forever,
Ray. I've been meaning to ask, how's
the job hunt going?

                    RAY
Not so well. I've had the usual
problems; no driver's license, no
experience, no real references, and of
course there's the problem with my
mask.

                    SALLY
I've always meant to ask about that.
Is it a religious thing?

                    RAY
No. Nothing like that. It's just a
decision I made a long time ago. It is
a code I have to follow. I can't take
it off in public, ever.

                    SALLY
That's really the problem isn't it.
I'll be honest with you, there is no
way I would have let you anywhere near
my kids wearing that mask, if you
hadn't showed up out of nowhere to save
us from that fire.

                    RAY
I just happened to be at the right
place at the right time. I'm sure any
other person would have done the same.

                    SALLY
Rescuing a bunch of panicked school
kids from a burning bus is no small
feat. I just hope someone out there
will look beyond your mask and see the
good man inside.

                    RAY
          Let's just hope I get to rescue some
          rich CEO sometime. Maybe he'll give me
          a chance.

EXT. ANTON DAVORIK'S CORPORATE HEADQUARTERS -- DAY

Anton Davorik's corporate headquarters is a large
skyscraper in the middle of a large southern city. It has
a slightly sinister appearance.

INT. ANTON DAVORIK'S OFFICE -- DAY

Anton's office is a large open room with a huge desk in the
center in front of a large open window overlooking the rest
of the city. There is a large corporate symbol on the
floor that appears to be a large Viking helmet with the
words "Strength. Will. Passion. Power." Encircling the
logo. His desk is empty save for a large computer monitor
and a intercom system. The far side of the office has a
two floor spilt area. The top area is filled with tons of
book shelves filled with many leather bound tomes and
laboratory equipment. The bottom floor area has tons of
computers and other high tech gadgets.

Currently seated at his desk is ANTON DAVORIK. He is a
sharply handsome man with a devilish grin. He wears the
finest suits money can buy since he is secretly the
wealthiest man in the world. He is powerful, charismatic,
and has an obviously sinister edge to him.

                    ANTON DAVORIK
          Well it looks like Velasquez didn't put
          the sword on Ebay after all. That
          saved us at least triple his asking
          price.

                    RUPERT MALTHEON (O.S.)
          You know the only other guy who would
          have bid in that price range was that
          software guy.

                    ANTON DAVORIK
          Yes, of course I know that. He would
          have wanted it for use in his Dungeons
          and Dragons game with that movie
          producer friend of his.

                    RUPERT MALTHEON (O.S.)
          That reminds me. You promised to get
          me an invite to their game.

                    ANTON DAVORIK
          You can play later. We've got work to
          do. I'm still waiting on that T.T.S.
          report. You had better have it soon or
          I'll let the Comtesse recruit you into
          her Foot-soldier program.

RUPERT MALTHEON walks into the shot from off-screen. He is
short and fat. He wears an Hawaiian print t-shirt and is
your stereotypical computer nerd minus the glasses. He is
carrying a burned DVD.

                    RUPERT MALTHEON
          I told you it isn't easy hacking into
          Heaven's intranet. They've got fire-
          walls that Hell never even thought of
          having. It was more difficult than I
          think you realize.

                    ANTON DAVORIK
          I take it that you have my report?

                    RUPERT MALTHEON
          You would have had it 5 minutes ago if
          you had gotten me that faster burner.

                    ANTON DAVORIK
          You just want it for those extra-
          dimensional Dr. Who episodes you
          discovered.

                    RUPERT MALTHEON
          Hey, you made a ton of money off those
          programs I pirated from that parallel
          dimension. I told you Xena and Power
          Rangers were going to be smash hits.

                    ANTON DAVORIK
          And you've been well compensated for
          that. None of that matters anyway now
          that I have this report. If my sources
          are correct, I can begin my hostile
          takeover bid sooner than expected.

Anton places the DVD into a slot in the desk and smiles when the screen changes to display the report.

> RUPERT MALTHEON
> Are we a go?

> ANTON DAVORIK
> I think we have our target. The Total
> True Souls report has proved to be more
> useful than I could have hoped.

Anton pushes a button on the intercom.

> ANTON DAVORIK (CONT'D)
> Christine, would you be a dear and
> contact a Mr. Gun from the special
> consultant file. Tell him I need to
> meet with him to discuss a contract and
> related fees.

Anton sits back in his chair.

> RUPERT MALTHEON
> Do I need to send word to the Comtesse?
> She's eager to begin any sort of new
> project.

> ANTON DAVORIK
> Why not? Gun will no doubt ask a
> pretty penny for his services. Plus it
> never hurts to get the jump on the
> competition.

EXT. CITY STREET -- EVENING

Ray is walking home from work. He has some shopping bags in his hands filled with groceries. Suddenly a police car pulls up with sirens blaring and lights flashing. They pull up behind him as a voice blasts over a bullhorn.

> SGT. ACKERMAN (O.S.)
> Drop the bags and turn to face the
> wall! Hands where I can see them.

Ray drops his groceries spilling them on the ground. He quickly turns against the wall and puts his hands on it. He has done this before.

Two police officers, SGT. ACKERMAN and SGT. RODRIGUEZ exit
the patrol car with guns drawn. Sgt. Ackerman is a young
officer fairly new to the area. Sgt. Rodriguez is an older
cop who has patrolled this area for years.

                    SGT. RODRIGUEZ
          Oh for crying out loud. Ray, is that
          you?

Sgt. Rodriguez lowers his gun and holsters it.

                    RAY
          Yes, Sgt. Rodriguez. It's me.

                    SGT. RODRIGUEZ
          Put your gun down, Ackerman. This is
          Ray. He's a local boy. He's not one
          of our suspects.

                    SGT. ACKERMAN
          You sure about that, Rodriguez? He's
          got a freaking mask on and he's
          carrying bags of loot.

Sgt. Rodriguez walks over to the groceries and holds up a
carton of crushed eggs.

                    SGT. RODRIGUEZ
          I don't think this is what was stolen
          from that bank.

                    RAY
          Can I turn around now, officers?

                    SGT. RODRIGUEZ
          Of course, Ray. I'm sorry about that.
          Some masked guys just hit the credit
          union hard a few blocks from here. You
          had better high-tail it off the street
          to keep from getting confused as a
          suspect again.

                    SGT. ACKERMAN
          How are you so sure he's not a suspect?

                    SGT. RODRIGUEZ
          Cause, Ray is good people. He helped
          us shut down a mess of local gang

bangers here last summer. This kid is
great in a fight.

                    SGT. ACKERMAN
How come I never heard about it?

                    SGT. RODRIGUEZ
Do you think the desk jockeys like to
read about masked vigilantes busting up
local drug rings that the detectives
couldn't crack?

                    SGT. ACKERMAN
You got a point. Get off the street,
Batman. Be glad I didn't Baker Act you
for being a masked freak.

                    SGT. RODRIGUEZ
Don't pay him any mind, Ray. I know
about luchadores from my folks. They
used to say that you guys protect us
all from the things the police were
afraid of. I've just never heard of
one in America.

                    RAY
As far as I know. I'm the only one.
Maybe I should just give up and head
south.

                    SGT. RODRIGUEZ
There's a thought. The weather is too
hot for me down there. I got to say,
though, I know this neighborhood might
not be much, but its a damn site better
than it was before you helped clean it
up. I'm happy you're here. Just keep
you head down until we catch these
thugs.

                    RAY
Will do... And Sergeant, good hunting.

The police get back into their patrol car and it pulls away
fast. Ray starts to pick up his groceries.

EXT. ALLEY -- NIGHT

Ray is walking by an alley when he hears a scream from
within. Inside we see a YOUNG GIRL being cornered by two
VAMPIRES. Ray walks up behind them.

                    RAY
          There's only one thing I hate about
          this town, all the damn vampires.

The vampires turn to face Ray and the girl looks slightly
relieved.

                    RAY (CONT'D)
          What's the matter? 80's vampire flicks
          too clichÈ? Maybe we should think more
          modern.

Ray starts circling the vampires and they close to battle.
Ray quickly crosses to a pile of old furniture that has
been thrown out in the alley. He quickly breaks off a
chair leg.

                    RAY (CONT'D)
          I think we should do this Tarantino
          style.

Ray rolls into one of the vampires and plunges the
sharpened point of the chair leg into his heart. The
vampire slowly turns to dust. As the other vampire roars
in anger.

                    RAY (CONT'D)
          I don't think I'll ever get used to
          that.

Ray grapples with the other vampire and rolls him to the
ground. He is about to impale the vampire with the chair
leg when the young girl grabs his hand. She has incredible
strength as she is also a vampire. She grabs Ray by his
wrist and pulls him into a head lock.

                    RAY (CONT'D)
          I'm having some serious deja vu here.

Ray quickly stumbles out of the hold and turns on the girl.
He pulls a rosary from his pocket and wraps it around the
vampire girl's neck as he reverse her hold on him. She
begins to choke as smoke pours off the rosary where its

holy energy is burning her. The vampire girl's head
finally comes off as her body turns to dust.

                    RAY (CONT'D)
          I will definitely never get used to
          this.

The other vampire runs out of the alley and changes into a
bat and flies away.

                    RAY (CONT'D)
          Well that's Ray with two falls out of
          three. Not too bad for a sparing
          match.

HAWK and AMANDA walk into the alley. Hawk is the head of a
Bureau 13 strike team situated in Ray's city. Hawk wears a
trench coat and carries all manner of monster-slaying
equipment on him including a very LARGE SWORD and several
guns. Amanda is young special agent on his team. She is a
highly trained High-school aged gymnast that specializes in
hand to hand combat with monsters. She wears a skin-tight
cat-suit and carries a wooden crucifix with silver
sharpened end.

                    HAWK
          Damn it, Ray, I thought we asked you to
          stop attacking the vampires. You've
          just spoiled this whole stakeout. You
          let the one slip away.

                    AMANDA
          Who knows what trouble that one that
          got away will cause? We could have
          trailed these three back to their hive
          and dusted the whole nest.

                    RAY
          I'm sorry to have spoiled your hunt. I
          didn't realize that Bureau 13 was in
          the habit of letting vampires stalk
          innocent civilians.

                    HAWK
          We knew she wasn't an innocent
          civilian. You should have, too. I
          should haul you in for obstructing
          justice, but you know I can't do that.

                    RAY
Especially since your organization
doesn't even officially exist. Where's
the rest of your cronies, Hawk? I
figure that three vampires would need
at least five of your people.

                    AMANDA
I could have taken them all personally,
given half a chance. I wouldn't have
let one slip away.

                    HAWK
That's enough Agent Winters. There's
no need for us to fraternize with this
vigilante. Listen, Ray, I know you're
trying to do the what you feel is
right. The thing is, the good old US
of A has monster busting covered. It's
not like it is south of the border. We
keep a tight wrap on all things unusual
and anything that gets witnessed gets
thrown into the next Hollywood
blockbuster. Shoot! My team alone is
responsible for two hit tv shows and
three of the top ten movies of all
time.

                    RAY
Your last one didn't do nearly as well
as the first two.

                    HAWK
We had poorer quality surveillance on
that assignment. That's not the point
though, Ray. Something big is going
down and you're just going to get in
the way. All I'm asking is that you
keep your head down so you don't get
caught in the cross fire. We'd been
tailing these bozos for three nights.
We had hoped to get back to their lair
and pacify them come daybreak.

                    RAY
How many civilians would have died
while you waited?

                    HAWK
Some losses are acceptable when you
look at the big picture, Ray. If
someone stupid had wandered into this
trap of theirs, he would have been an
tragic casualty. The plus side would
have been, that we would have gotten
all three or even their whole damn crew
to stop many more deaths.

                    RAY
I just can't be willing to let one
innocent die. It's the code of the
luchadore.

                    AMANDA
You're not even Mexican. Do you even
speak a lick of Spanish?

                    RAY
You don't have to be Spanish. It's
just more common there.

                    AMANDA
So what's with the Rosary? You have to
have a lot of faith for that to work.
Are you Catholic?

                    RAY
Sort of. I once saved a church full of
people from a horde of zombies. Your
precious Bureau was nowhere to be
found. I couldn't save everyone, but I
saved most of the people. The church
sends me some money and keeps me
supplied with weapons of lordly might.
I wish I didn't have to rely on the
compassion of others so much. Maybe I
could apply for a government grant.

                    HAWK
Cute, Ray. Just keep your head down
the next few days or it might get shot
off.

Hawk speaks into his EAR PIECE.

                    HAWK (CONT'D)
          This is Hawk. We're heading out.

Hawk and Amanda run out of the alley and into a waiting RV.
It speeds off into the night. Ray sighs as he picks up the
rosary from the pile of ash. He looks closely at the pile.

                    RAY
          I wonder if they let you be turned, so
          they could hunt some bigger fish. It
          just shouldn't be this way.

EXT. A SMALL TOWN CHURCH -- NIGHT

BEGIN DREAM SEQUENCE

There is a small church surrounded by flames. The sound of
screams can be heard. There are menacing shadows of
shambling human forms grabbing helpless victims. There is
a quick glimpse of Carlotta being swarmed by zombies. The
a pale eyed zombie face roars directly onto the screen.

END DREAM SEQUENCE

INT. RAY'S APARTMENT -- DAY

Ray sits bolt upright in his bed. He is visibly shaken by
yet another dream. He rolls over and sees a half eaten
chili-dog beside the bed.

                    RAY
          Why do I do this to myself?

The phone rings on the nightstand.

                    RAY (CONT'D)
          This is, Ray

                    MARONI (ON PHONE)
          Hey, Ray. I got you an audition with
          the N.W.E. You might have a good shot
          at it.

                    RAY
          .... Really, Maroni? No kidding? I'll
          be there as soon as I clean up...

INT. ANTON DAVORIK'S OFFICE -- MORNING

Anton is sitting at his desk looking at his recently
acquired gladius sword. FREDDY VELASQUEZ is standing on
the other side of the desk. Freddy is a young man dressed
in khakis and a polo shirt. Very business casual, he looks
like your average joe.

                    FREDDY
          I think you'll find it to be completely
          genuine. As if I've ever sold anything
          that wasn't.

                    ANTON DAVORIK
          I expected more from the Sword of
          Alexander, the one used to cut the
          chains of Prometheus. It hardly weighs
          an ounce, but still it could cut the
          chains of Hephaestus, let alone the
          Gordian knot.

                    FREDDY
          That's what the guy in Calcutta told
          me. That shaman guy in Tanzania did
          his mojo on it and said it was forged
          from a rock that fell from the sky.
          Carbon dating was inconclusive, as
          usual, but my sources have concluded
          that it's the real deal.

                    ANTON DAVORIK
          Amazing! Worth every penny, thank you
          again, Mr. Velasquez.

                    FREDDY
          My pleasure, Mr. Davorik, but please
          call me Freddy. Everybody else does.

                    ANTON DAVORIK
          You have always provided me with the
          best of materials, Freddy. You'll find
          your payment in the usual account
          already.

Freddy pulls out a palm pilot and clicks a couple of times.

                    FREDDY
        Um, I can't believe I'm saying this,
        but I think you put in a little too
        much.

                    ANTON DAVORIK
        Not at all, Freddy. I'm just going to
        need to increase my arsenal by about
        tenfold over the next few days. Do you
        think there's any chance of you filling
        my shopping list?

Anton places the sword into a sheath on the desk. Then he
hands Freddy a long sheet of paper.

                    FREDDY
        For that kind of money, I can get a lot
        of these things. Sure, I can make this
        happen. Give me a day or two and the
        artifacts will start flowing in. Once
        word gets out I'm on the hunt, the
        sellers usually find me.

                    ANTON DAVORIK
        If any of those private collectors
        refuse to part with some of the more
        obscure artifacts then please don't
        hesitate to inform me. I will gladly
        see to it that Comtesse Campanella will
        pay them a visit to negotiate an
        equitable solution.

                    CHRISTINE (ON INTERCOM)
        Mr. Davorik, Mr. Gun is here to see
        you.

                    ANTON DAVORIK
        Send him in, Christine. Mr.
        Velasquez... Freddy, I think you should
        be on your way. I know you and Gun
        have a history of sorts. Didn't you
        try to buy his silver?

                    FREDDY
        Yeah, about five years ago, I heard he
        was thinking of hanging it up. I
        figured he's still got about 3 pieces
        left, so I figured I'd offer up a bid.

The guy's a psycho. He offered to let
me buy two of the pieces if I let him
shove the third piece in a very
uncomfortable place.

           ANTON DAVORIK
Then I suggest you use the back exit.
It's upstairs through the library. You
had better be quick about it.

Freddy rushes up the stairs and disappears into the stacks
of books. GUN enters the office from the front door. He
wears a cowboy duster and cowboy hat pulled down slightly.
He keeps the duster buttoned up past his mouth so the only
thing one can see of him are his eyes. He walks up to
Anton's desk and sits down without saying a word.

           ANTON DAVORIK (CONT'D)
Welcome, Gun. I see it's not just a
name, but also your nature.

           GUN
Cut the crap, Anton, what's the job?

           ANTON DAVORIK
Good, we'll cut to the chase. Time is
money after all. I recently obtained a
report of the Total True Souls in the
world.

           GUN
And I'll just bet, Paris Hilton isn't
on that list.

           ANTON DAVORIK
You would be correct. There is only
one true soul left over the age 25.
Hell's been after him for a few years.
I think your services would accomplish
this task much more efficiently.

           GUN
That would be right. Except, I ain't
cheap.

           ANTON DAVORIK
Of that I have no doubt. I read up on
how you've used those 30 pieces of

silver throughout your very long
career. Was it true that you let one
go for a bottle of brandy and a night
with a Persian whore?

                GUN
It was a good bottle of brandy and a
very good whore. Of course the rates
have gone up since then. I've got two
slugs left in old "Pain" here. I don't
intend to let them just casually go to
waste.

            ANTON DAVORIK
Gun, I'm here to make you one hell of
an offer. You know that I sold my soul
to Satan many years ago, to get ahead
in the business world. Well that
worked out sublimely. Now that it's
getting near payback time, I've decided
I've got a better payment plan.

                GUN
You want to redeem yourself and win
your soul back? You know that only
works in the movies.

            ANTON DAVORIK
You are correct. There is nothing that
I can do to win back my soul without
giving up everything I have
accomplished. No, I intend to use my
business skills and complete the task
that Satan has been unable to do. I
intend to damn the last true soul. My
products and programs are already
damning as many souls as hell's demons
do directly. Desperate Housewives
alone nearly tripled my soul income
last year. I just need to tip the
balance a little in my favor.

                GUN
Are you saying what I think you're
saying?

                    ANTON DAVORIK
Yes. I intend to take over Hell and
become the new dark lord of the
universe. It's the ultimate hostile
takeover.

                    GUN
And you intend to do this by damning
the last true soul?

                    ANTON DAVORIK
Exactly. Of course Bureau 13 will have
to be kept from interfering. I've also
made sure that all the other do-gooders
of note in the world are occupied.
That just leaves me with one simple
question.

                    GUN
You want to know how much it'll cost
you for "Pain" to deliver the damnation
bullet on your target.

                    ANTON DAVORIK
Exactly.

                    GUN
Ok. Here's my cost. 9 billion dollars
deposited into an account of my
choosing and when you get in charge of
Hell you purge me from the roll of the
damned.

                    ANTON DAVORIK
9 Billion? That's insane. Just 40
years ago you only charged the CIA 300
million for that deal in Texas.

                    GUN
That was different. I didn't like his
politics. Besides I don't think either
side is going to let you get away with
this. You meet the first part of my
price and I may be able to live a long
comfortable life on some island and
never have to worry about what comes
next.

                    ANTON DAVORIK
          Very well. It will take me a few days
          to come up with that kind of money. I
          suggest you work on figuring out how to
          get to the target.

Anton turns the computer monitor around and its a picture
of the Pope in a Popemobile in front of a large crowd.
Gun leans forward to get a good look.

                    GUN
          I never would have guessed.

Anton pushes the intercom button on his desk.

                    ANTON DAVORIK
          Christine, my dear, would you please
          contact the Comtesse and tell her to
          start Operation Smash and Grab. Tell
          her to have no mercy on our
          competition. She should, however, show
          some composure when dealing with our
          own insured interests. No need to bite
          the hand that feeds her.

INT. SMALL GYM WRESTLING RING -- DAY

Ray is wrestling a couple of guys in a tag team match.
This is near the end of the match and Ray trips one
wrestler and leg locks the other wrestler. He does a flip
and slams the other wrestler into the ground on top of the
original wrestler. MARONI, Ray's agent, is visibly
impressed. He elbows the N.W.E. TALENT SCOUT.

                    MARONI
          I told you the kid's got moves.

                    N.W.E. TALENT SCOUT
          We've already got enough masks for the
          Hispanic audience. How's he look
          without it?

                    MARONI
          Um... Great. Yeah, great. Thing is
          the kid's got an idol that was some
          sort of big time masked wrestler back
          in the 50s. I think he's going to
          insist on the mask.

                    N.W.E. TALENT SCOUT
          Well, I understand these legacy types.
          He'll want to make his idol proud and
          never lose a fight. That doesn't make
          good drama. Since he won't lose the
          mask, he'll have to start as a bad guy
          and lose a lot. If he's cool with
          that, I think we can make a deal.

EXT. OUTSIDE OF THE GYM -- DAY

                    MARONI
          I think we've got you a deal. The only
          real question is are you willing to
          lose the mask?

                    RAY
          You know I can't do that.

                    MARONI
          Yeah, I figured. Then we've got
          another wrinkle. If you won't loose
          the mask, they're going to want you to
          play the bad guy card. You know what
          that means?

                    RAY
          I get better dialogue?

                    MARONI
          No it means, you're going to have to
          lose. I mean lose a lot. I know that
          probably upsets you more than losing
          the mask.

                    RAY
          I'd be paid to lose. Don't they always
          play to win.

                    MARONI
          This isn't exactly a sport anymore,
          Ray. It's a show. It's spectacle.
          The viewers in the crowd want drama as
          well as good wrestling. That means
          you've got to have story lines, and
          plot. Which means the bad guys have to
          lose, unless they become really
          popular.

                    RAY
          Can I think about it?

                    MARONI
          It's good money. I think it's the best
          offer you're going to get. This
          industry understands the mask. This is
          all you're going to have. The local
          group has dried up. We're talking TV
          spots, action figures, and the whole
          works eventually. You've got talent,
          Ray. Don't let it slide because of
          some stupid good luck charm.

                    RAY
          Let me think about it. I'll get back
          to you in a couple of days.

                    MARONI
          Don't wait too long. They want an
          answer by Friday.

EXT. JEWELRY STORE -- DAY

A large group of zombies being led by COMTESSE CAMPANELLA
are breaking into a jewelry store. The Comtesse is an
elegant lady of Italian nobility, and the Zombie Queen.
She wears a long black dress and stands out against the
hordes of zombie soldiers that surround her. These ZOMBIES
are dressed as soldiers from a variety of eras. Most of
the zombies carry guns and move in fighting formations.
Alarms sound as the zombies smash into various cases and
load up large bags of jewels some of which seem very
valuable. They stagger up to the Comtesse and drop some
bags at her feet. She picks up a large necklace.

                    COMTESSE
          I'm so glad Anton has decided to let us
          take this action. I did so have my
          heart set on diamonds.

EXT. A SMALL SIDE STREET -- DAY

Ray walks by hears the sound of a scuffle within the side
street. He looks on as he sees MARLIL being beaten up by a
YOUNG RUFFIAN. Marlil is a older man wearing a beat up
long coat and a large ankh necklace. He also carries a

large walking staff that he is using to try and defend
himself with.

Ray begins to rush to his aid, but remembers his
admonishment from Bureau 13. He hesitates and looks to see
if help is on the way.

He waits a couple of moments, debating jumping to the old
man's rescue.

                    RAY
          Damn! No cops. No government goons.
          I've got to do something.

Ray rushes into the alley and tackles RICHARD, the young
ruffian. Ray flips Richard onto his back. He is taken
back a bit when he realizes the thug turns out to be one of
his students from the recreation center.

                    RAY (CONT'D)
          Richard? Is that you? What do you
          think you're doing?

                    RICHARD
          I'm sorry, Ray. I needed the money and
          he seemed so helpless. I didn't
          think...

                    RAY
          What do I do with you? If I turn you
          into the police you'll be in jail. If
          I let you go that will be too easy.
          Don't you realize what you've done?
          You follow this road and your life is
          nothing but hardship and torment.

                    RICHARD
          Your life isn't? I just wanted to get
          out of this slum. I'm destined for
          greater things. I'm not going to be
          some loser scraping his way in life,
          like everyone else in this place,
          including you.

                    RAY
          Get out of here, Richard. If I ever
          see you do anything like this again,
          you'll be in jail so fast, your head

will spin. Go home and talk to your
folks, maybe they can give you a little
more positive direction.

The young thug runs out of the alley. Marlil gets up
surprisingly quickly for one that had been apparently been
beaten so bad.

                    MARLIL
          I was beginning to think you were never
          going to help me. I guess I was very
          wrong about you. You do realize that
          that child has more issues than a stern
          talking to can help.

Ray turns around and looks at Marlil. Marlil is now
standing strongly with his staff at his side. There seems
to be a slight glow around his staff.

                    RAY
          Who the hell are you?

                    MARLIL
          I the hell am, Marlil the Magnificent,
          High wizard of the Grand Council. I am
          here to test your abilities. You will
          be needed on a quest soon, Sir Ray. I
          am here to see if you are worthy of
          this task.

                    RAY
          Just what I need, someone with a
          Gandalf complex. Listen, sir, I've got
          enough on my plate right now. I'm sure
          there's someone else who is the
          rightful King of Gondor.

                    MARLIL
          Your reference is lost to me. Do you
          not know to expect the coming of a
          wizard? One who will grant you a gift
          of power and allow you to assume the
          role of a champion of the people.

                    RAY
          I don't know what game you're playing.
          If this is some sort of Bureau 13 game,
          I'm certainly not interested. I'm

going to be getting my life in order.
I've already told you guys, I'll stay
out of your way, but if I see any
innocent person being hurt I'm not
going to stand idly by.

                    MARLIL
          That is most honorable of you; however,
          I do not belong to those pretenders at
          Bureau 13. There is no need to be so
          aloof. Can you not see that I am a
          true wizard?

                    RAY
          That's nice, but I've got better things
          to do right now. You just head on back
          to your sci-fi convention and I'll head
          on home and well pretend this never
          happened.

Ray walks away from the alley as Marlil sighs. He then
uses magic to summon up a mist that swirls around him as he
slowly fades into it.

EXT. WAREHOUSE -- DAY

The last of the escaped vampires from the other night is
rushing into a warehouse. He is jumping from shadow to
shadow to avoid the burning sunlight. Hawk and Amanda are
in close pursuit, but trying to stay out of sight. The
vampire looks back over his shoulder to check if he's being
followed. Once he's sure of it he ducks into the
warehouse. Hawk holds a hand to his earpiece.

                    HAWK
          This is, Hawk. Agent Winters and I are
          in position outside the VesztesÈg
          Cendest·rs warehouse by the docks. Our
          pigeon just went home to roost.

                    AMANDA
          It looks like M and Harold are ready.

                    HAWK
          Agent M you go in the back and flush
          them out our way. Have Agent Kettle
          throw up some protection hexes on the
          back door so they have to run into

                    Agent Winters and I. We're the ones
                    trained for Vamp fighting.

EXT. WAREHOUSE REAR -- DAY

Two figures approach the back door of the warehouse. One
is AGENT M, a man in an all Black suit with sunglasses. He
carries with him a small silver GUN that looks very alien
in design. The other is HAROLD, a young boy in his early
teens. He wears a black robe and very thick glasses. He
carries a small WOODEN WAND and a old LEATHER BOUND TOME.
Agent M touches his earpiece as well.

                          AGENT M
                    This is M. We are in position at the
                    rear entrance. I'll get the kid to
                    work on the wards. As soon as they are
                    up, we'll head into the nest.

                          HAROLD
                    Give me a minute to find a ward against
                    vampires. I had a "hold spell"
                    prepared.

Harold flips through the large book.

                          AGENT M
                    I don't have all day, kid. The sun
                    will be down soon. That will tip the
                    odds in their favor.

                          HAROLD
                    Don't rush me. I'm no good under
                    pressure.

                          AGENT M
                    I'll bust your ass myself if you don't
                    get a move on.

                          HAROLD
                    Got it.

He waves his wand at the door. A blue glow of energy
covers the door as he traces a pattern in the air with his
wand.

                          HAROLD (CONT'D)
                    "Habui Potoir! Nosferatus Repelicari!"

There is a pop of energy and the blue glow on his wand blasts forth and forms a wall of solid blue light on the door.

                    AGENT M
          I can't argue with that. Now let's go
          put a cap in Kid Dracula's ass. Hawk,
          this is M. Harold... I mean Agent
          Kettle, got the ward up. The back door
          is secure we're going in to flush them
          your way.

The pair charge into the house.

EXT. WAREHOUSE -- DAY

Hawk and Amanda have taken positions on both sides of the
front door. Hawk has drawn his sword and Amanda holds her
silver stake. They wait for a moment. Then they begin to
show signs of concern.

                    HAWK
          M, report. Have you engaged the enemy?

                    AMANDA
          Harold, this is Amanda, are you there?
          Did the spell work?

                    HAWK
          This is bad. I want all team members
          to report in now. M? Harold? I need
          a sit rep on the double.

                    AMANDA
          They're not responding. Do we go in?

                    HAWK
          Of course we do. This is what the
          Bureau gets for not sending in those
          reinforcements I asked for.

                    AMANDA
          Did they say why they didn't send
          reinforcements?

                    HAWK
          Something about a zombie outbreak in a
          major city. All their resources were
          being tied up.

                    AMANDA
          Oh hell. That will make one hell of a
          movie when they lock it down.

                    HAWK
          M, Harold, we're coming in. Watch your
          fire.

They charge into the warehouse. There are the sounds of a
scuffle and sword fighting. Then there is a scream as we
see the sun set over the warehouse.

INT. RAY'S APARTMENT -- NIGHT

Ray walks into his apartment and is surprised to find
Marlil sitting on his couch.

                    RAY
          Who are you and how did you get in
          here?

                    MARLIL
          I told you I'm a wizard and to answer
          your second question, I'm a wizard.
          Now can we please dispense with this
          ridiculousness and get down to the task
          at hand.

                    RAY
          All right, I believe you can pick
          locks. I believe in magic because I've
          seen a lot of spooky crap. I've even
          seen that Bureau kid work some movie
          level special effect type stuff.

                    MARLIL
          That kid and those like him are
          tampering with energies far out of
          their control. There are only a few
          true wizards in the world. Those fools
          who need spell books are merely a step
          above stage magicians.

                    RAY
          So what makes you so special? That kid
          did some impressive stuff.

                    MARLIL
          I can banish demons to the pits of the
          abyss. Then I can summon forth that
          very same demon and have him do my
          bidding and you are more impressed by a
          child making a wand light up.

                    RAY
          At least he's shown me some stuff. If
          I'm supposed take your word, Obi-wan,
          and follow you to Mos Eisley then
          you're going to have to show me some
          force powers.

                    MARLIL
          The reference is lost on me, but I
          comprehend its meaning.

Marlil closes his eyes whispers under his breath. A
swirling mass of energy fills the room which morphs into a
winged demon with curled ram horns and grey skin. The
demon howls with rage and begins to leap toward Ray. Then
it sees Marlil on the couch and quickly regains its
composure. It walks over to Marlil and sits daintily on
the couch next to the wizard and crosses his legs.

                    WINGED DEMON
          Hello, Marlil. Long time no see. I
          hope this isn't another surveillance
          job?

                    MARLIL
          No, Belihicior. I just needed a quick
          show of strength to convince this young
          fool I am a powerful wizard.

                    WINGED DEMON
          So you use the old "summon an arch-duke
          of the Seventh Circle of Hell" trick to
          convince the boy to be a champion of
          good. You always were as subtle as an
          impalement. I guess this is a
          recruitment drive due to the recent

unpleasantness. The fool seems slack-
jawed now. I assume I am dismissed.

                    MARLIL
Once I send you back. You think I'm
old enough to be that addled? I'm not
going to dismiss you from service until
after you return to the pit. A free
demon would eviscerate us both.

                    WINGED DEMON
So very true, Marlil. Forgive me, but
It simply wouldn't due to not try and
disembowel the wizard that banished me.
What I don't understand is why you're
trying to train another champion when
you've already given your gift of power
to another champion. I'm also quite
certain that the High Council of
Wizards would not approve of this
blatant interference, let alone
summoning a demon to this plane of
existence.

                    MARLIL
You've spoken enough, Belihicior. I
banish you back to hell. Once there
you are free from my service until such
time as I summon you to this plane
again.

The demon simply vanishes.

                    RAY
I think I'm suitably impressed.

                    MARLIL
I hoped as much. Sadly, the demon
wasn't lying about several things.
First, I am getting old, even for a
wizard. My power has faded
significantly. Secondly, I have given
my gift to another champion long ago.
We will need another wizard to grant
you his gift. Lastly, he is correct
about the High Council not approving
this. They have pledged to never again
interfere in the affairs of the world.

Therefore we cannot count on the
assistance of any wizard on the High
Council or any that follow its
teachings.

           RAY
What did he mean by "recent
unpleasantness?"

           MARLIL
A great evil is on the rise. Creatures
that used to cling to the shadows are
starting to operate in the open. I
only hope your Bureau 13 is going to
contain all these breakouts of
supernatural entities. Still, the
forces of light will need a champion to
seek out the source of this evil and
destroy it.

           RAY
So why me?

           MARLIL
You know the power of The Order of The
Luchadore. You are one of a breed of
heroes that defend the world openly
against the tides of darkness. Even
without a proper guide, you have fought
well.

           RAY
That still doesn't answer my question.
Why not the Son of Santo or Blue Demon?
Why not Mil Mascaras or even Superzan?
I don't even speak Spanish.

           MARLIL
I once gave my gift of power to a great
man. He was the great El Santo. He
used his powers to help found the order
of luchadore. His mantle has passed
down from generation to generation.
Each Santo has fought bravely against
the forces of darkness. Each
eventually fell gallantly.

                    RAY
          I know all this. I saw the movie.

Ray holds up a DVD of El Santo and the Devil's Ax.

                    RAY (CONT'D)
          I thought it was Merlin who gave El
          Santo's descendant the mask.

                    MARLIL
          That was the screenwriter's
          interpretation. Merlin was a truly
          powerful wizard that gave a gift of
          power to a champion of his own
          choosing. You may have read something
          about that. I sought out El Santo when
          my time came.

                    RAY
          Then am I getting Excalibur or the mask
          of El Santo?

                    MARLIL
          Neither, those gifts are claimed. Only
          those of the bloodline of the chosen
          champion may use them. Your blood is
          new. You will need a wizard to grant
          you a mantle of power.

                    RAY
          But you said no wizard would grant me a
          gift, due to their Prime Directive.

                    MARLIL
          Your reference is lost on me, but I
          understand its meaning. I merely
          stated that no wizard that supports the
          Council would help us. There is one
          other that might.

                    RAY
          Why do I get the feeling that I'm not
          going to like this guy.

                    MARLIL
          You must do your best to try to find
          him agreeable. He holds the key to
          your receiving a gift of power. You

would do well to be mindful in his
presence.

                    RAY
        I'm still not sure how much of this I
        fully believe. Aren't there other
        luchadores available for the job?

                    MARLIL
        I thought you might say that.

Marlil mumbles something and his staff glows slightly.
Then Ray's phone rings. Ray rushes over to answer it.

                    RAY
        Ray here.
            (IN SPANISH)

                    EL HIJO DEL SANTO (O.S.)
        Hello, Ray. This is El Hijo Del Santo.
            (IN SPANISH)

                    RAY
        But I don't speak Spanish.
            (IN SPANISH)

                    MARLIL
        My spell makes it so. It will not last
        long.

                    EL HIJO DEL SANTO (O.S.)
        The luchadores are in Mexico City and
        we are busy with El Satanico and his
        alien minions. We only wish we had
        someone to spare.
            (IN SPANISH)

                    RAY
        I'm trying to follow the code of the
        luchadores, but it is so hard here. In
        America the police chase me, no place
        will hire me, and I have no friends or
        family.
            (IN SPANISH)

                    EL HIJO DEL SANTO (O.S.)
        My father told me of a young gringo
        luchadore that spent time with him one

summer. My father wanted him to
succeed in his dream of being the first
American Luchadore so he let him leave
his camp to pursue his dream.
          (IN SPANISH)

                    RAY
I came home to find my parents dead and
my town plagued with zombies.
          (IN SPANISH)

                    EL HIJO DEL SANTO (O.S.)
If only I had a dollar for every
luchadore that told me that. Ray, you
will do well for my father's memory and
for the memory of your parents. Live
by the code of the luchadore and you
will prevail.

                    RAY
Hey, you speak English.

                    EL HIJO DEL SANTO (O.S.)
A little, I grow weary of translation
spells when it is easier to just speak
English.

                    RAY
Thanks. Once again I owe a lot to a
Santo putting me on the path of a
luchadore.

                    EL HIJO DEL SANTO (O.S.)
Good hunting to you!

                    RAY
And to you.

Ray puts down the phone and looks at Marlil.

                    RAY (CONT'D)
Let's go find that wizard.

                    MARLIL
Oh, he's very hard to miss.

EXT. WAREHOUSE REAR -- NIGHT

Amanda crawls over stacks of boxes, she is clearly injured
and is bruised and bleeding. Her left arm hangs limply at
her side, obviously broken. She is panting and trying to
use her earpiece.

                    AMANDA
          This is Special Agent Amanda Winters,
          to any available Bureau 13 personnel.
          Strike Team Orange Smoothies has been
          all but eliminated. Team leader Hawk
          has been terminated by hostile vampiric
          forces. Agent M and Agent Harold
          Kettle are MIA. I am requesting an
          emergency EVAC from any Bureau mage or
          psi-op that can hear me. Is anyone
          receiving me? Isn't there anyone on
          the line?

A shadowy form rises into view leading a group of zombies
behind her. Amanda raises her sword with her good right
hand. She struggles with fighting as many she can but they
wind up swarming her. The screen fills with zombies and we
loose sight of Amanda.

EXT. LYCAEON'S SHOP -- NIGHT

Marlil and Ray appear outside of a Palm Reader shop in a
suburban area in a burst of blue energy. The big neon sign
says "Palm Reader and Cosmic Center." Marlil laughs at the
sign and leads Ray into the building.

INT. LYCAEON'S SHOP -- NIGHT

Lycaeon's shop is filled with strange and unusual jars.
There are also tons of books surrounding the place. There
is a curtained off area to the side of the shop. The
curtain is open and reveals a small table, complete with a
crystal ball on top. An ancient man sits behind a sales
counter. The man has a beard that looks like it could hide
a family of beavers. His hair is wild and he wears clothes
in the style of a hippy. The old man stands as they
approach the counter.

                    MARLIL
          There is no need for the glamour,
          Lycaeon. We are not easily influenced

mortals ready to have their hard earned
money plucked form them by the likes of
you.

                    RAY
I thought you said we had to be nice to
this guy.

As Ray speaks the ancient man's image begins to fade like
the color fading from an old painting. The illusion
disappears to reveal LYCAEON. Lycaeon is a young man that
exudes arrogance and a roguish charm. He is actually
wearing a tie dyed shirt and jeans. Lycaeon inspects
Marlil and Ray with a small measure of contempt.

                    LYCAEON
You don't have anything on me, Marlil.
I haven't broken any of the Council's
rules. I'm just putting the customers
in contact with those that can help
them.

                    MARLIL
I'm sure there's some rule somewhere
about selling magical tomes to mortals.

                    LYCAEON
These books? None of these have any
real power to them. You know that
school over in the UK buys most of the
stuff that leaks away from Council
members, those magi wannabes from
Bureau 13 take the rest. These are all
just pyramid power and crystal junk. I
just keep it around because it makes
the chics happy.

                    RAY
Did you just say, "chics?"

                    LYCAEON
I'm sorry, masked man. Us all powerful
wizards are talking here. You mind
just zipping your lip while the
grownups chat?

                    MARLIL
Lycaeon, I'm not here to punish you for
any transgressions. I'm not here to
try to get you to come back to the
Council. I'm here to ask for your
help.

                    LYCAEON
It really is that bad, isn't it. I had
a feeling when some of the stuff
started getting on the actual news it
was getting rough. The news crews are
having a tough time saying "the victims
suffered sever upper body trauma," over
and over again. I figured that the
Bureau or S.A.F.E. would put a stop to
all that.

                    MARLIL
Apparently it is too much for them.

                    LYCAEON
And the Council is being too
pretentious to get up off its ass, as
usual.

                    MARLIL
I do not like the words, but your
connotation is accurate. That is why I
have sought out a new champion.

                    LYCAEON
What is it with you and masked men?
First the wrestler, then the cowboy
with the silver guns and the Indian
sidekick. You know, Ariela still
thinks he was a poor choice of
champion.

                    MARLIL
She was a foolish wizard and only
granted him a magic horse. That horse
did not avail him when true evil came
for him.

                    LYCAEON
So this is the your pick? I suppose
you think I'm just going to give him a

gift of power and then wait for the
Council to rain toads upon my shop or
something.

                MARLIL
No. I intend for you to assist us in
stopping whatever evil is about to
befall our world. I also would like
you to stop selling glamoured items in
your shop.

                LYCAEON
Well I've got an important client
coming in shortly and I have no time to
run off on some quest. Besides I'm not
much into wrestling. I was thinking
that I would look for some hot
Amazonian babe to grant a gift of
power. Then she could thank me for it
over and over again.

                RAY
Great, not only is he a jerk, he's also
a pervert.

                LYCAEON
I'll have you know I'm a true gentleman
when it comes to the ladies. I always
make sure their needs come first. I'll
grant you, that being a wizard makes
that a little easier, with love spells
and the like. That still doesn't make
my meeting with Chastity Vale any less
important.

                RAY
Chastity Vale?

                LYCAEON
Her parents were hippies. She's a
total goth chic into dead poets. I'll
put her in contact with an air spirit
in the guise of Lord Byron and she'll
be very very grateful. Man, I love me
the goth chics.

                         MARLIL
          That's enough, former apprentice. You
          know as well as I that the evil is
          growing. We must prepare Ray to take
          the mantle of hero. Once he is ready,
          I'm sure you'll come up with something
          creative for his use.

There is a scream from outside. All three of them race to
the door. Lycaeon vaults over the counter to keep pace
with the others.

EXT. LYCAEON'S SHOP -- NIGHT

Ray, Lycaeon and Marlil exit the shop. A few doors down
zombies are closing in on CHASTITY VALE. Chastity, is a
goth girl that looks like she could easily be one of the
Suicide Girls.

Ray doesn't hesitate and leaps into the crowd of zombies.

                         MARLIL
          These are extraordinarily constructed
          undead. The aura of black magic is
          strong in the area.

Ray gets slammed into a wall by two zombies.

                         RAY
          So what does that mean?

                         LYCAEON
          What Marlil is trying to say in typical
          enigmatic wizardly fashion is that
          these are really strong zombies. They
          are pretty close to an alpha zombie or
          a powerful necromancer. You're going
          to need fire for them.

Lycaeon raises his hand and a staff appears in it. He
speaks some gibberish words powerfully and flames shoot out
from the end of his staff, incinerating the nearest zombie.

                         LYCAEON (CONT'D)
          How about a little fire, scarecrow?

Ray runs over to the burning zombie and rips his flaming
arm off. He then turns to face the other zombies with the
flaming limb.

                    RAY
          Quoting old films while you fight.
          Maybe there is hope for you.

                    LYCAEON
          Ripping off a flaming zombie arm to use
          as a weapon. Maybe there is hope for
          you, too.

The fight is now clearly too much for the zombies. Marlil
and Lycaeon each incinerate one more zombie. While Ray is
a whirl of motion, he spins and ignites 4 more undead
zombies himself while managing to keep them all away from
Chastity.

                    CHASTITY
          Thank you. You saved me.

                    LYCAEON
          Well it was nothing, Chastity.

Chastity runs past Lycaeon and runs into Ray's arms.

                    CHASTITY
          If there's any way I can thank you, you
          just let me know. I do things that can
          make a porn star blush.

She smiles and runs her hands on Ray's shoulders. Lycaeon
glares at the luchadore.

                    LYCAEON
          You had better get home, young lady.
          It's obviously not safe for you here
          tonight.

                    MARLIL
          Lycaeon, I will place a protection
          charm on the young lady. I think you
          and Ray need to see if you can spot the
          source of the energy manifesting these
          undead.

                    LYCAEON
          Fine. We'll go find the puppet master
          while you "lay hands" on my horny goth
          girl.

                    RAY
          I'm sorry, Lycaeon. I did not intend
          for her to see me as her savior. You
          are obliviously much more powerful than
          I could ever hope to be.

                    LYCAEON
          If you think I'm jealous of a punk like
          you, Ray, you've got another thing
          coming. I just used up a ton of juice
          back there and didn't have time to get
          a proper glamour on. They always fall
          for the brooding angst ridden tough guy
          in the heat of the moment. That is,
          until the sardonic vaguely mysterious
          scoundrel type wanders back onto the
          scene.

P.O.V. LYCAEON'S SHOP -- MOMENTS LATER

A shot from the scope of a rifle from a rooftop across the
way of Lycaeon and Ray wandering into Lycaeon's shop.

EXT. ROOFTOP -- NIGHT

The rifle we were looking through is lowered to reveal the
jigsaw puzzle of a figure that is GLENDALTON FRIGARDSON.
This Frankenstein-like mountain of a zombie is patched
together from dozens of dead soldiers. He smiles and lifts
the rifle back into sniping position.

INT. ANTON DAVORIK'S OFFICE -- NIGHT

Anton is monitoring his computer while sipping a glass of
wine with his free hand. Comtesse Campanella walks over to
his desk.

                    ANTON DAVORIK
          These figures are even more prosperous
          than I could have hoped. It's a good
          thing we divested ourselves of the
          insurance companies last year. Your
          zombie apocalypse is doing wonders for

my security firms. The American people
are still convinced this is some sort
of race riot.

                    COMTESSE
I have brought out Glendalton to handle
our strategic operations. I'm seeing
to most of the larger operations
personally.

                    ANTON DAVORIK
I don't mind you taking a little off
the top to indulge your personal
tastes, Comtesse. Just don't get too
carried away. We've still a little
ways to go to reach Gun's price.

                    COMTESSE
What is your plan once you damn the
last true soul? Do you really believe
they will make you the new lord of Hell
just like that?

                    ANTON DAVORIK
Heavens, no. The demons and devils
will have a massive civil war with
Lucifer's loyal soldiers on one side,
and those with vision on my side. When
it's over and we've won, I'll split the
Earth up with you, the Marquis, and
I'll probably have to bring in Yang to
control Asia.

                    COMTESSE
Are we going global now? I thought you
were strictly concentrating on North
America.

                    ANTON DAVORIK
South America is being pestered by
Satanico and his alien horde at this
point. I would love to claim he was a
part of my plan, but the truth is, he
just started operations at a very
fortunate time for me.

                    COMTESSE
          That half-devil will be defeated by the
          luchadores.

                    ANTON DAVORIK
          You are of course correct. I'm just
          hoping that he keeps them busy for a
          few days while we complete our
          operations here.

                    COMTESSE
          Well I'm going to go have a light
          supper. I've ordered some Chinese.

                    ANTON DAVORIK
          Enjoy your meal. I think after that
          we'll see about sending you to
          Kentucky. The National Guard is busy
          defending the major cities, so I think
          Fort Knox might be vulnerable. If we
          hit it hard and fast we could increase
          our fund exponentially.

                    COMTESSE
          So after dinner I'll head for the
          hills.

INT. RAY'S APARTMENT -- NIGHT

Ray and Lycaeon enter the room and find Marlil watching an
El Santo DVD on the screen.

                    RAY
          He was a great man. He taught me so
          much about the luchadore code.

                    MARLIL
          El Santo was indeed a great man. He
          told me that you fled his training
          after only a few weeks in Mexico. Then
          you disappeared for years until I
          stumbled across you in a newspaper
          account about the schoolchildren and
          the bus.

                    RAY
          I missed my home. My mother and father
          did not go with me to Mexico. I was

                    young and I didn't understand why I had
                    been chosen. When El Santo sent for me
                    my parents were pleased...

INT. RAY'S CHILDHOOD HOME -- DAY

BEGIN FLASHBACK

Ray's FATHER and MOTHER are standing at a door waving at
the car that is driving YOUNG RAY away from them. Young
Ray's face is concealed by a glare on the windshield.
Ray's parents turn and head back into the home.

                         RAY (V.O.)
                    That was the last time I saw them. I
                    don't know if they had any idea about
                    what sort of a world they had sent me
                    into.

EXT. A LARGE APARTMENT -- DAY

Following behind Young Ray, he is seen led into a spacious
and tastefully decorated apartment. On the walls are
abstract paintings and other works of art fill the
apartment. EL SANTO, the famous Mexican wrestler, walks
into the room wearing his famous silver mask and a white
suit. He walks up to young Ray and shakes his hand.

                         RAY (V.O.)
                    It was there I met El Santo, the
                    greatest luchadore of all time. He
                    explained to me about the code and how
                    I was the first "Gringo" he had ever
                    heard of receiving the call.

EXT. A SMALL MEXICAN TOWN -- DAY

Young Ray and El Santo are being treated like kings in this
small Mexican town. People are throwing money and offering
them gifts. Many beautiful women are looking upon the
luchadores with lustful eyes.

                         RAY (V.O.)
                    Santo showed me how the people of his
                    country worshipped him for his good
                    deeds. Their generosity was an amazing
                    sight.

EXT. A SMALL MEXICAN TOWN -- NIGHT

Young Ray, now masked, fights a group of vampires in the
town. He circles them as El Santo coaches him from the
side. Ray grabs one in a head lock then pulls him into a
sleeper hold. He then plunges a stake into it's heart.
The other vampires try to close in on him, but he quickly
steps back. El Santo tosses him a sword and Ray brandishes
it like a fencer. He swings viciously at the remaining
vampires.

                    RAY (V.O.)
          Santo also taught me about the
          "Vampiros" and other creatures of the
          darkness. For two weeks we fought
          monsters almost daily. During the day
          he feasted and enjoyed the company of
          many beautiful women. By night he
          fought as the greatest warrior of them
          all.

EXT. A SMALL MEXICAN TOWN -- DAY

Young Ray is getting back on a bus and waving goodbye to El
Santo and the people of the town.

                    RAY (V.O.)
          In the end, I just missed home. I
          didn't speak Spanish very well. I
          didn't have nearly the training El
          Santo had, I felt like a hindrance
          rather than a help. Besides I missed
          my parents.

                    LYCAEON (V.O.)
          I'll bet there was a girl back home,
          too. There would have to be, to turn
          aside all of those lovely SeÒoritas.

                    MARLIL (V.O.)
          Lycaeon, be silent. I am anxious to
          know why Ray left training for his
          calling so soon.

EXT. A SMALL TOWN CHURCH -- MORNING

We see the sun rising in the distance and bathing the small
church in sunlight. Carlotta is there playing soccer with
some other girls outside the church.

                    RAY (V.O.)
          Lycaeon's right. There was a girl.
          She had this dark hair that seemed to
          swallow light. I wanted to just watch
          my fingers disappear into the blackness
          as they ran through her hair. I used
          to watch her play soccer with some of
          the other girls from town. I never
          even bothered to learn her name.

                    LYCAEON (V.O.)
          Wow, there is hope for you. You loved
          her and left her without even learning
          her name. And I thought I was heart
          breaker.

                    RAY (V.O.)
          No you don't understand. I loved her,
          but never had the courage to ask her
          out or even say one word to her. I
          vowed that when I returned from Mexico
          I would ask her to be mine. It would
          be up to her if I would become a true
          luchadore or not.

EXT. A SMALL TOWN CHURCH -- NIGHT

There are flames surrounding the church and hordes of
zombies are running rampant through the streets of Ray's
hometown. The bus is turned on its side and we see Ray
climbing out of it. He begins to battle the zombies with
various wrestling moves.

                    RAY (V.O.)
          When I returned home, zombies had
          overrun the town. The survivors of the
          initial attack had fled to the church.
          It was built to keep out the Spanish
          soldiers long ago. It was holding up
          fairly well against the zombies.

                    LYCAEON (V.O.)
          Let me guess. She was one of the
          zombies?

                    RAY (V.O.)
          No, she was locked in the church. I
          don't know what came over me. Seeing
          those people in danger... No...
          Seeing her in danger. I knew then that
          I had to battle evil wherever and
          whenever I could.

END FLASHBACK

INT. RAY'S APARTMENT -- NIGHT

                    RAY
          I knew I couldn't ask her to live the
          life of a luchadore's wife. I beat
          back the zombies and by morning a team
          of Bureau 13 agents arrived to mop up.

                    LYCAEON
          A day late and a dollar short. I think
          that's the Bureau's motto.

                    MARLIL
          Bureau 13 is a strong force for good in
          this land. I feel though that are
          unable to handle the coming evil.

                    LYCAEON
          Coming evil? We've got zombies running
          amuck in large metropolitan areas. I'd
          say the evil is here.

                    MARLIL
          I'm not so sure. The zombies are merely
          a branch of this tree. We must find
          the root of this evil.

                    LYCAEON
          Tree metaphors? Come on, Marlil, that
          was a stretch even for you. Shit, can
          the enigmatic wizard act, will you?
          What you and I need to do is conjure up
          a map of zombie outbreaks and figure
          out what they want.

                    RAY
          Or we could just turn on the news.

Ray walks over to the television and turns it on. Lycaeon
smiles at the luchadore.

                    LYCAEON
          Wizards and technology don't mix well.
          Something about the mystical energies
          we throw around and electricity don't
          mix very well. It's a very oil and
          water kind of thing.

                    RAY
          But Marlil was watching a DVD when we
          came in.

                    MARLIL
          We can use technology, it's just
          usually easier to avoid it.

                    NEWSCASTER (ON TELEVISON)
          ... as the rioting in Louisville poured
          into the countryside. The National
          Guard has been ordered to attack the
          rioters and calm the situation before
          it gets any worse.

                    SOLDIER (ON TELEVISON)
          Looting in the wake of the riots is
          still our primary concern. It's like
          everyone thinks it's an excuse for a
          shopping spree.

                    NEWSCASTER (ON TELEVISON)
          That's it for the national wrap-up.
          Once again in local headlines, the area
          around Parkside Mall is now under
          martial law as the unexplained rioting
          continues.

Ray turns off the television.

                    RAY
          Someone needs something and they are
          willing to use an army of the dead to
          get it.

                    LYCAEON
That or a lot of people are unhappy
with the winner of Dancing with the
Stars.

                    RAY
I thought you said wizards didn't watch
television.

                    LYCAEON
I said magic and technology don't mix
well. I never said anything about
watching sexy starlets doing the tango.

                    MARLIL
It would appear that our services are
required yet this evening. How far
away is this Parkside Mall?

                    RAY
About 45 minutes walking. Maybe 30
minutes if we run.

                    LYCAEON
Um, Ray. You still don't get the
wizard thing do you?

                    MARLIL
If we transubstantiate, Lycaeon, we
will be very vulnerable once we arrive.
Both you and I have already used much
of our magical reserves this evening.

                    LYCAEON
Marlil, don't you realize that almost
every mall is located on a lay line
hub? Once we're there it'll only take
a minute or two to be at full charge
again.

                    RAY
Then I guess I'd better cover you guys
for a couple of minutes when we arrive.

                    LYCAEON
I'm still not quite ready to leave my
life in your hands, masked man. I'm

bringing the modern wizards best
friend.

                    RAY
          What's that?

                    LYCAEON
          Hopefully you'll never find out the
          hard way.

                    MARLIL
          Enough! Can you turn that television
          of yours back on, Ray? As soon as I
          can see our destination I will send us
          there.

Ray turns on the tv. The sound of screams flood out of the
television. Marlil begins making gestures in the air as
his staff glows. Ray, Lycaeon and Marlil fade from view as
their mystical energy causes the television to explode.
Lycaeon quips as they dissolve.

                    LYCAEON
          I told you magic and technology don't
          mix.

EXT. PARKSIDE MALL -- NIGHT

The large strip mall is filled with ZOMBIE SOLDIERS
ransacking various shops. They are primarily looting a
sporting goods store and a another jewelry store. Ray,
Lycaeon and Marlil appear in a blast of blue energy with
the sound of a thunderbolt.

                    RAY
          Looks like we're too late to save
          anyone. This place is trashed.

Marlil leans heavily on his staff to catch his breath.
Lycaeon lifts his staff in the air to gather energy.

                    LYCAEON
          There's so much black magic in the air
          it will be difficult to get some clean
          energy. I didn't think about that.

                    MARLIL
          Ray will make sure no harm will come to
          us until we have regained some of our
          might.

                    RAY
          I'll do my best.

                    LYCAEON
          Here comes your chance. They've
          spotted us.

ZOMBIE SOLDIERS turn and stagger at the winded wizards.
Ray strides forward to confront them in a fighting stance.

                    RAY
          So let's see who's brave enough to try
          me first.

A zombie lunges at Ray. He sidesteps him and locks him in
a half-nelson. He quickly snaps the zombie's neck and
drops him to the ground. The others attempt to swarm him.

                    LYCAEON
          These are some of the most organized
          zombies I've ever seen. Are they using
          some sort of advanced tactics?

                    MARLIL
          They must be soldiers of the Zombie
          Queen. Most zombies you have faced
          were nurses, office workers and the
          like. The Comtesse likes to use
          trained warriors. She grants them
          extra power so they might retain some
          of their former skills along with their
          undead strength.

                    LYCAEON
          In other words, Ray is up shit's creek;
          and once they finish with him, we're
          the main course.

Ray breaks free from the pile of soldiers and grabs one by
the zombie's legs. He swings him in a circle causing it's
knife to slice the heads of several other zombies. He then
throws the zombie he holds into another crowd of zombies.

                    RAY
          Lyc, is fire needed again? Snapping
          the necks seems to be working.

                    LYCAEON
          Snapping the necks is fine. I'm not
          sure I'm comfortable with you calling
          me Lyc though. Ray! Watch your back!

A zombie reaches up for Ray from the pile of bodies. Ray
kicks the zombie's head and breaks its neck.

                    RAY
          Thanks for the heads up. They've
          really torn into the sporting goods
          store. Looks like they've hit the
          jewelry store, too. They haven't
          touched the television store. Will the
          magic animating them not work there?

Ray reports while still battling with the occasional
zombie. These are more like the regular zombies including
soccer moms, mall walkers and store clerks. They are not
nearly as hardy as the early cadre of soldier zombies.

                    MARLIL
          Magic still works around technology.
          It is a puzzlement why they would avoid
          such a spectacle of a store. Zombies
          are usually attracted to things they
          were attracted to in life. Television
          I understand is a big priority among
          these people.

                    LYCAEON
          He's right. Maybe it's got some sort
          of protection. If you get a shot, see
          if you can throw a zombie near it. I'd
          like to see what happens.

                    RAY
          I'll do my best.

A gunshot rings out as a bullet nearly misses Ray. The
sound of rifle fire fills the parking lot as Ray looks
around.

                    RAY (CONT'D)
Has the Bureau finally arrived?

                    LYCAEON
I don't think so. They seem to be
aiming for you. Watch yourself.

                    RAY
It's more soldier zombies. They've
armed themselves with weapons from the
sporting goods store. They've got
hunting rifles.

                    LYCAEON
Now that's just not fair. Zombies can
barely swing a club, let alone fire a
gun. You charged up yet, Marlil?

                    MARLIL
I am once again able to wage battle.
Let us engage these soldiers with
eldritch fire.

                    LYCAEON
A simple yes will do. Do you always
have to talk like you're freaking Ken
Brannagh?

A bullet narrowly misses Ray as he notes the name of the
television store.

                    RAY
Stand in front of the store. The
zombies seem to be afraid to shoot in
its general direction.

                    LYCAEON
Marlil and I will start some barbecue
action, you corral them into our flame.

                    RAY
Right.

Ray launches himself into the zombies and begins shoving
them toward the wizards. Lycaeon and Marlil raise their
staffs and blast out a fountain of flame and crackling
energy. The zombies are incinerated.

                    RAY (CONT'D)
I've got to admit. Having wizards
around sure makes life interesting.

                    LYCAEON
I still don't get why they were afraid
to open up on us in front of this
store.

                    RAY
I'm curious about that, too. Computers
R Us over there didn't fair so well.
The jewelry store got trashed. I
wonder if someone is financing some
sort of zombie army.

                    MARLIL
The Comtesse, might just do such a
thing.

                    LYCAEON
You mentioned her before. Who is she?

                    MARLIL
The zombie queen, Comtesse Campanella,
was once a powerful wizardess. She
turned her powers toward the dark arts
and it is she who invented the magical
study of Necromancy. Long since turned
into a creature of the undead herself,
she uses her magical skills to create
outbreaks of zombies to seize political
power and influence in smaller
countries around the world. She usually
moves on when she has achieved her goal
or the food supply is gone.

                    LYCAEON
You mean when all the people are dead.

                    MARLIL
You would correct.

                    RAY
Let me guess, Bureau 13 has made some
money off of her attacks with the
Romero movies.

                    MARLIL
          Your allusion has no meaning to me, but
          I believe you are correct in your
          assumption that the Bureau has thwarted
          her before.

                    RAY
          So the question is really, why hasn't
          the Bureau stopped them this time?

Several police cars arrive. Ray, Marlil and Lycaeon look
for an easy way out of sight.

                    LYCAEON
          I really don't think we're cut out for
          covering this up. This is really a bad
          time for Bureau 13 to talk a vacation.

                    RAY
          Can't you send us out of here with
          magic again?

                    LYCAEON
          In a minute. I don't think we've got
          that long though.

                    POLICE OFFICER (O.S.)
          Hold it right there! Put your hands
          where I can see them.

                    LYCAEON
          Marlil, you got enough in you to get us
          out of here?

                    MARLIL
          I do not yet have the energy for
          transubstantial locomotion. I do
          believe that illusion is, however, a
          field you excel at.

                    LYCAEON
          Good idea.

Lycaeon whispers into the wind and his words take shape on
the wind in the form of a very scantily clad Chastity
walking towards the police. She begins to dance
suggestively while she removes articles of clothing. The
police stare stunned.

Ray, and Lycaeon help Marlil into the darkness between the stores.

                    POLICE OFFICER (O.S.)
          Hey, they've gone.

                    SECOND OFFICER (O.S.)
          Who cares? The area is secure and
          we've got us a show.

Chastity finishes her erotic dance. She turns away from the police cars and fades into nothingness.

EXT. RAY'S APARTMENT -- MORNING

Ray once again wakes up in a cold sweat. Marlil is sitting in meditation and Lycaeon walks into the room.

                    LYCAEON
          You know, Ray. You really should clean
          this place up if you're hosting guests.

                    RAY
          I have to say that the last thing I
          ever expected yesterday morning was to
          suddenly have two wizard roommates.

                    LYCAEON
          Well I got to say, I wasn't expecting
          to be staying in some fixed income
          place with a masked wrestler and my old
          mentor, either.

                    RAY
          He trained you?

                    LYCAEON
          Well, not exactly. Once I was born the
          seventh son of a seventh son, the
          Council of Wizards took me for
          training.

                    RAY
          How old were you?

                    LYCAEON
          It was my thirteenth birthday. My
          parents were extremely surprised.

                    RAY
I'll bet. You don't hear about that
kind of thing in the newspaper.

                    LYCAEON
Especially back in 1792.

                    RAY
1792?! That makes you over two hundred
years old!

                    LYCAEON
I like to think I don't look a day over
170.

                    RAY
That's insane.

                    LYCAEON
That's one part of the wizard gig, a
very long life span. Marlil over there
is well over 700 years old.

                    RAY
That's so crazy.

                    LYCAEON
Well as I was saying, the Council took
me to the great sage Abdul Al-Hazzared.
Unfortunately he had a couple of young
serving girls that were supposed to
remain virgins.

                    RAY
So the horny wizard thing isn't just an
act.

                    LYCAEON
It's a way a life. Abdul went mad a
few years later and turned to dark
magics. It's the only reason I was
allowed to continue training. My
deflowering of his servant girls kept
him from summoning some ancient evil or
other.

                    RAY
So you saved the world with a bang.

                    LYCAEON
Be fair, it was a threesome. Boy, I
wish I could use that line. "Come on,
girls. The only way to save the world
is a three way."

                    RAY
Very classy. I still can't believe
that you saved the world.

                    LYCAEON
Every wizard has saved the world at one
time or another. Most of the time
they've really only saved a city or
province or something.

                    RAY
That's more than I've ever done.

                    LYCAEON
I've seen you in action a few times
now. You saved a few dozen civilians
last night alone. Who knows, maybe one
of them will save some other people in
turn.

                    RAY
You mean like saving the mother of a
future great hero, or something like
that.

                    LYCAEON
Exactly. The one law of the universe
is that no matter what you do, it comes
back on you tenfold. Save a few people
and if you did it right, they will help
a few hundred people.

                    RAY
What if you accidentally save a bad
person.

                    LYCAEON
Then hopefully they reward you in a
creative way. I really enjoy rescuing
bad girls.

Marlil's eyes blink open and he stands.

                    MARLIL
Apparently you enjoy conjuring
illusions of those you've rescued as
well. I have to admit it was a very
compelling illusion.

                    LYCAEON
You, old lecher. It's not hard to pull
off a good illusion with a photographic
memory.

                    MARLIL
Since you were telling Ray your life
history, perhaps you should tell him
about the cost of being a true wizard.

                    RAY
Cost?

                    LYCAEON
That's the real problem. Long life for
us means a lot of good-byes. I've
buried dozens of friends and allies. I
buried all of my brothers and sisters
when a demon called the Crotoan came
for my home town.

                    MARLIL
That's where I found him. That same
demon had destroyed my home in 1588. I
wasn't about to let him destroy another
city in my beloved New World.

                    RAY
1588? Crotoan? Your talking about the
Lost Colony.

                    MARLIL
Jamestown was my home. I was the first
wizard of European ancestry to be born
in North America. The Council refused
to accept me for years.

                    RAY
     (Getting dressed)
This is some crazy stuff.

                    LYCAEON
Anyway, Crotoan wakes up. He starts
eating the town and Marlil shows up and
blasts his ass with a huge fireball.
It was like a sign from above!

                    RAY
I imagine it was.

                    LYCAEON
I knew then that I had to return to the
teachings of magic. I just had to know
how to blow stuff up with a flick of
the wrist and a few magic words.

                    RAY
I've seen a few other wizards use some
pretty potent stuff. That kid with the
local Bureau team.

                    LYCAEON
That kid is no real wizard. He just
got into a real good school with some
rudimentary magic.

                    MARLIL
A true wizard's power comes from his
strength of will. We have no real need
for wands and magical tomes. Our
staves store extra energy for those
crucial times of need.

                    RAY
No midicholorians then?

                    LYCAEON
Nice. He's right though. Magic is an
art and not a science. That's why
learning it from books or Charmed isn't
going to get us a ton of wizards.

                    RAY
So what's the deal with Bureau 13?

                    LYCAEON
They were formed sometime in the 1800s.
A secret service type agency to protect

the United States from monsters and
things that go bump in the night.

                    RAY
They have any real wizards?

                    MARLIL
The Council of Wizards refuses to allow
any interference with the mortal world.

                    RAY
Oh yeah, that prime directive thing.

                    LYCAEON
Good analogy.

                    RAY
I thought so.

                    MARLIL
All you need to know about the Bureau
is that they are not apparently
operating at full capacity. Something
is keeping them from acting. We must
have ourselves a hearty breakfast and
then begin our quest to find the cause
of this evil.

INT. ANTON DAVORIK'S OFFICE -- DAY

Anton is perusing the books in the library section of his
office. Rupert is downstairs working on the large
computers.

                    ANTON DAVORIK
I'm quite pleased with our results.
Wouldn't you agree, Rupert?

                    RUPERT MALTHEON
I guess so, boss. The reports I'm
getting from Hell are saying that some
big time devils are refusing to
acknowledge our recent damnation
totals.

                    ANTON DAVORIK
They will once I bring them the
ultimate prize. There are always

holdouts in any takeover bid. What's
amazing to me is that some of the
younger devils have already signed
allegiance to me and we haven't even
made a formal announcement.

While he is talking, Anton casually walks down the stairs
and heads back to his desk. He sits and checks the
monitor.

                    RUPERT MALTHEON
          I just got off of ASKGOD.ORG, it seems
          heaven's a little concerned about the
          zombie attacks. Not to mention El
          Satanico and his aliens are being
          pretty openly active down in Mexico and
          South America.

                    ANTON DAVORIK
          What have you found about Bureau 13?

                    RUPERT MALTHEON
          They are down and almost out. Using
          our inside man we managed to take out
          about 70% of their active agents in
          less than 24 hours. They're pulling in
          reservists and retired agents to try
          and hold their HQ.

                    ANTON DAVORIK
          Wonderful news, Rupert. We're about
          10% above plan in this venture.

                    RUPERT MALTHEON
          I'm going to get that new core system
          with the holographic storage?

                    ANTON DAVORIK
          I'm afraid I feel we should invest a
          little more in Mr. Velasquez's toys to
          upgrade our arsenal. All we need now
          is some do-gooder to come in at the
          last minute and spoil things.

                    RUPERT MALTHEON
          I do have a report about one operation
          that came to a premature end. Reports
          are that some local cops actually

                    managed to defeat one group of the
                    Comtesse's soldiers.

                              ANTON DAVORIK
                    Really? I find that hard to believe.

Anton pushes the intercom button.

                              ANTON DAVORIK (CONT'D)
                    Christine, get me the Comtesse please.
                    I'd like a word with her.

                              RUPERT MALTHEON
                    Your pulling her out of the field to
                    come here? She's not going to be happy
                    about that.

                              ANTON DAVORIK
                    I'm merely going to re-prioritize our
                    plan of attack. If someone has hurt
                    our business interests in an area, I
                    think we should send in a headhunter.
                    Don't you?

EXT. RECREATION CENTER PLAYGROUND -- DAY

Ray and Sally are talking while Marlil and Lycaeon try to
not look conspicuous.

                              SALLY
                    I'm sorry, Ray. With all the rioting
                    we're closing down for a few days. I
                    'll call you when things settle down.

                              RAY
                    It's ok, Sally. I was actually coming
                    to ask for a few days off anyway.

                              SALLY
                    Did you get another job? That
                    wrestling thing I heard about?

                              RAY
                    Word travels fast, but no. I don't have
                    another job. As for the wrestling
                    thing, I'm still thinking about that
                    offer. I really just wanted to make
                    sure you and the kids were safe.

                    SALLY
          We'll be fine, Ray. Those guys you're
          with seem kind of shady, are you sure
          you're not in any trouble?

                    RAY
          Don't worry about me. I can take care
          of myself. Besides those guys are old
          friends, I'm just showing them around
          town for a few days.

                    SALLY
          Be careful, Ray.

                    RAY
          You, too.

INT. JEWELRY STORE -- DAY

Marlil and Lycaeon are standing beside the store that was
robbed the night before. They begin chanting and casting.
Ray stands back and watches.

After a moment there is a strong glow that rises from the
ground and forms a misty cloud of energy over the wizards.

                    MARLIL
          As I expected. This was no random act
          of zombies.

                    RAY
          What did you two do?

                    LYCAEON
          It's a simple tracking spell. We were
          looking for directed magical energy and
          boy did we find it.

                    RAY
          What does that mean?

                    MARLIL
          The meaning is clear. Someone is using
          these zombies for simple finance.

                    LYCAEON
          It does seem odd, to use that kind of
          magical power for breaking and
          entering.

                    MARLIL
          They also draw undue attention to these
          acts. They risk the wrath of many
          forces.

                    LYCAEON
          The Inquisition wasn't that long ago.
          Do you really think someone is ready to
          start a new one?

                    RAY
          If someone is building a zombie army,
          maybe they just need financing for
          weapons.

                    LYCAEON
          You may have hit the nail on the head.
          They could build their army and destroy
          the United States in one fell swoop.

                    MARLIL
          Comtesse Campanella has in the past
          done similar acts. She usually only
          attempts this in small island nations
          though. Grenada and Haiti being the
          most recent.

                    LYCAEON
          Yeah, usually they report it as some
          sort of revolution or military
          operation. I've just never heard of
          her hitting anything this big before.

                    RAY
          Maybe she's got someone pushing her
          along.

                    LYCAEON
          Possible, but they'd have to be pretty
          powerful to pull the zombie queen's
          strings.

EXT. SHOPPING CENTER -- DAY

A quick shot done as a newscast of ZOMBIES attacking a
mall. The headline across the bottom of the screen says
"ACTION NEWS BREAKING STORY: RIOTING INTENSIFIES DOWNTOWN"

The camera is jerking about violently and ends with a
zombie face grabbing the camera and the screen going blank.

INT. ANTON DAVORIK'S OFFICE -- DAY

Comtesse Campanella leans over Anton's desk slinking like a
vixen.

                    COMTESSE
          Anton, you know I have better things to
          do than be here.

                    ANTON DAVORIK
          I want to know what happened the other
          night. We've only had one attack
          abbreviated and I want to know exactly
          what occurred.

                    COMTESSE
          I'm not sure myself. I was checking a
          fine sapphire that one of my
          lieutenants had brought me. That
          section was not under my direct
          control.

                    ANTON DAVORIK
          So you delegated the operation to one
          of your minions. What did he say.

                    COMTESSE
          I don't delegate. I merely allowed
          Glendalton to handle that wing, as it
          was merely a shopping center and would
          have little of any substantial value.

                    ANTON DAVORIK
          Glendalton... The mongrel? I still
          don't understand what he is doing in
          your service.

                    COMTESSE
          All those who have journeyed beyond the
          veil can be swayed by my abilities. He
          was surprisingly easy to control.

                    ANTON DAVORIK
         A being composed of thousands of dead
         soldiers... I can see how that would
         fall into your purview.

                    COMTESSE
         I will have him report to me directly
         on this incident. I assume the police
         were simply more organized than we
         expected. He was ordered to keep
         police casualties to a minimum, to
         maintain the rioting cover story.

                    ANTON DAVORIK
         My chief concern is how close this
         action was to our headquarters here. If
         there is a do-gooder, a rogue Bureau 13
         operative, a white hat, or worse a
         cape, than I want to know about it.
         The stakes are too high for a loose
         cannon to blow my plans to hell.

                    COMTESSE
         If we are finished here, I will go and
         speak to Glendalton presently. He is
         currently handling that operation at
         the airfield.

                    ANTON DAVORIK
         Just keep an eye on him. I've read his
         files. He occasionally exhibits bouts
         of pacifism and generosity. We can't
         have that at this critical juncture.

                    COMTESSE
         He is merely a puppet and I pull his
         strings. I will make sure there are no
         further mistakes. Then perhaps we can
         further discuss my position in the new
         hierarchy of hell.

EXT. AIRPLANE HANGAR -- DAY

Police cars surround a hangar with lights flashing. There
is occasional burst of machine gun fire from within the
hangar strafing the helpless police. Officers scramble for
cover constantly repositioning themselves for safety and to
try and get a clear shot inside.

Marlil, Lycaeon and Ray appear in a cloud of green smoke
near the edge of the combat. Marlil sits down, clearly
winded from the amount of energy he has just used.

              LYCAEON
You're getting too old for this,
Marlil. I told you to let me aid you
with the teleport spell.

              MARLIL
I will simply need a few moments to
compose myself. We did not know what
the situation was. I could not allow
both of us to be defenseless upon
arrival.

              RAY
That's why you brought me along,
remember. I think I can handle just
about anything they throw at us.

              MARLIL
You haven't seen anything yet. You've
fought some vampires and zombies. Have
you faced a true demon? Have you been
in combat with a six-armed Troll?
Let's not even speak of the Old Ones or
the Eldritch horrors that have brought
plagues and terrors on mankind for
centuries.

              RAY
I'm sorry, Marlil. You're right. We
should play it safe and keep one of you
guys charged up. I just want to feel a
bit more useful

              LYCAEON
Well you just keep hoping, Ray. I'm
still wanting to feel a bit more useful
when he's around, too. I haven't quite
mastered that old wizard tactic of
being one step ahead of the rest of the
world yet.

                         MARLIL
          It is merely being observant. You may
          both wish to step this way for a
          moment.

Ray and Lycaeon step towards Marlil assuming him to be in
some pain. At that very moment a series of gunshots
peppers the wall where they were standing and fills it with
holes.

                         LYCAEON
          See... One step ahead.

                         MARLIL
          I simply saw the weapon aiming in your
          direction. I suggest we keep to the
          shadows.

                         RAY
          The police have them bottled up inside
          the hangar. The problem is the cops
          don't know they can't be killed by
          bullets. I assume there's something
          important inside they want.

                         LYCAEON
          I'm not detecting any objects of power.
          Maybe its another money play.

                         RAY
          I'm just not used to zombies with guns.
          Not like I'm used to zombies at all.
          Vampires I've dealt with my hole life,
          but zombies only once before.

                         LYCAEON
          Right, you said that, and fancy pants
          over there told you that only the
          really powerful zombie leaders can have
          minions that use weapons. So whatever
          is in there is important enough to
          fight for.

                         RAY
          Which means we want to keep them from
          having it. So how do we get past the
          cops and the zombies? I'm not bullet-
          proof.

                    MARLIL
Not yet. Lycaeon, I think you should
place a "mask" on our luchadore.

                    RAY
I've already got one.

                    LYCAEON
No, he means a masking spell. It'll
simply make you blend in with the
background. If anyone looks directly
at you it'll break. Also, the minute
you physically contact another, it'll
dissolve.

                    RAY
Kind of like the Predator?

                    MARLIL
The reference is once again lost to me.
I do believe you understand. Lycaeon
will enhance your natural stealth. You
will sneak in and assess the foe. If
you feel you can act than take them.
If you feel overwhelmed then return and
fetch us to assist you.

                    RAY
You got it. Ok, Lycaeon, camouflage
me.

                    LYCAEON
I'll make the NRA proud. FOLIARO
KONTRAUOLIO FENESTRO!

Energy warps from Lycaeon's hands as it surrounds Ray.
Leaves and sticks circle him like a small tornado. Within a
moment the wind and energy dissipates leaving a blurred
form where Ray was standing.

                    RAY
I'm really invisible?

                    LYCAEON
Yeah, but you're not silent, so shut
it. Go in there quiet like and see
what's going on. We'll be waiting
here. Yell if you need a hand.

                    RAY
          Just make sure you're ready in case
          your masking spell doesn't work on
          zombies.

As we see the blur crouch and make its way toward the
hangar, Lycaeon turns to Marlil.

                    LYCAEON
          I don't know whether he's brave or
          stupid.

                    MARLIL
          There is always a fine line between
          those traits. Sadly it is the same
          with hero and villain.

INT. AIRPLANE HANGAR -- DAY

Ray's blurred form enters the hangar and we see zombie
soldiers occasionally firing from cover at the police.
Glendalton stands near the back of a plane overseeing the
offloading of a large crate.

                    GLENDALTON
          Soon, my soldiers, we shall face the
          foe on the battlefield instead of this
          simple defensive action. This crate
          has to be the one we seek for our
          mistress.

The blurred form of Ray steps closer to see what is in the
box. Glendalton sniffs the air as he approaches.

                    GLENDALTON (CONT'D)
          I smell you, wizard. Your invisibility
          cloak won't hide you for long. I've
          dealt with your kind before.

                    RAY (V.O.)
          I'm not a wizard, zombie master. I'm
          just here to make sure no one else gets
          hurt.

                    GLENDALTON
          I am not a zombie master. If you wish
          to avoid casualties I suggest you
          remove those mortal officers and leave

us to our work. My soldiers can not
die. It would be a shame to add those
noble police to my army.

                RAY (V.O.)
You're right. It would be a damn
shame. Surely as a former soldier you
understand they have to try to do their
job and arrest you.

                GLENDALTON
Foolhardy and ridiculous. Surely they
see their task can not be accomplished
with the materials at hand. They
should retreat and regroup.

                RAY (V.O.)
You obviously don't know the local
cops. Besides they don't know what you
are. These aren't monster hunting
professionals. They're just Joe
Policeman trying to make their city a
little safer.

                GLENDALTON
And who are you, I-am-not-a-wizard?
You obviously understand the situation.
Are you some negotiator from the
Wizard's Council? Perhaps you are one
of those Bureau agents we missed in our
cleansing operations.

Ray's blurred form steps right in front of Glendalton and
reaches out to touch him on the shoulder. When contact is
made Lycaeon's spell is broken and Ray returns to
visibility, like a paint by numbers coloring one color at a
time.

                RAY
I am Ray, a luchadore, and protector of
innocents. I can not allow you to
endanger any more lives.

                GLENDALTON
A Luchadore? Here? I thought you were
all in Mexico dealing with El Satanico
and his alien army.

                    RAY
          No. I am here, dealing with a zombie
          general messing with the police
          officers in my town!

                    GLENDALTON
          Then I'm afraid you will die.

Glendalton draws his gun to fire but Ray leaps on him
before he can raise the weapon. The other zombies turn to
aid Glendalton.

                    RAY

Come on, General. You going to let
your boys take your glory. I know you
weren't a desk jockey. Let's finish
this between us.

                    GLENDALTON
          Stand down, boys. This is between the
          mask and me. If he wins, you may
          return to the mistress. If I win we
          will feast on the heart of a noble
          adversary.

Ray and Glendalton once again grapple. Glendalton throws
powerful punches that Ray blocks or dodges. Ray is
throwing minimal punches but continually attempts to
grapple the large zombie.

                    GLENDALTON (CONT'D)
          You are an agile opponent.

Glendalton lunges at Ray, who deftly spins aside.

                    RAY
          You fight very methodically. You're
          telegraphing every move.

Ray lands a solid punch to Glendalton's chest. Glendalton
is unharmed by the blow and swings his own crushing fist at
the luchadore.

                    GLENDALTON
          You are daring to give me advice on how
          to fight?

                    RAY
          It looks like you've used a gun too
          long. You aren't going to be able to
          land a solid hit on me for hours.

Glendalton circles Ray and tries to grab him from behind,
but Ray uses a judo throw and flips the giant zombie onto
the ground. Glendalton rolls quickly to his feat and again
resumes a fighting stance.

                    GLENDALTON
          It's good thing I'm not mortal then.
          Too bad you'll tire long before I will.

                    RAY
          I'll let you know when I get tired.
          Sooner or later you'll over-lunge and
          then I'll get you in a hammer lock.
          Then it'll just be a matter of time
          before I figure out a way to separate
          your head from your neck.

                    GLENDALTON
          You're toying with me?

                    RAY
          Not really. I'm just waiting for the
          right time to make my move. I wouldn't
          dream of toying with you.

Glendalton drops his guard and starts to laugh loudly.

                    GLENDALTON
          My god, man. You've got balls of cold
          steel. I've never seen such valor.

Ray smiles and laughs too, as he lowers his guard as well.

                    RAY
          So, are you surrendering?

                    GLENDALTON
          No, I'm afraid I can not surrender as I
          have my orders. I can however order a
          strategic redeployment of my soldiers.
          We shall meet again, luchadore. Next
          time I will not yield the battlefield
          so easily.

                    RAY
          I wouldn't have it any other way. Keep
          up your left hand though, it was very
          hard not to keep punching your jaw.

                    GLENDALTON
          Soldiers, cease fire and vacate the
          area of operation. We are leaving.

The zombie soldiers holster their weapons and line up
behind Glendalton. He pours a potion from a canteen on his
belt into a circle around he and his zombies. They
disappear in a flash of light.

                    RAY
          That's not exactly how I expected that
          to go. Let's see what's in the box on
          the floor.

He walks over to the crate and opens it. Inside are
various paintings of extreme beauty and value.

                    RAY (CONT'D)
          All this for another robbery?

                    SGT. RODRIGUEZ (ON BULLHORN)
          All right throw down your weapons and
          come out with your hands on your heads.

                    RAY
          Sergeant Rodriguez! It's me, Ray!
          I've handled this situation! I'm
          coming out with my hands up!

EXT. AIRPLANE HANGAR -- DAY

Ray is talking to the two police officers, Sgts. Ackerman
and Rodriguez. Ray is not in handcuffs. Lycaeon and
Marlil are watching from a safe distance but within
earshot.

                    RAY
          ...the terrorists were after the
          paintings. They must've thought
          weapons were in the crate. When I came
          down through the skylight the
          terrorists went into a panic. They
          crawled out though a small hole in the
          back of the warehouse. I tried to stop
          them, but there were just too many of
          them.

                    SGT. ACKERMAN
          I'll believe that when my daughter is
          happy her dad is a cop.

                    SGT. RODRIGUEZ
          Look, Ray. We know some of the strange
          stuff that's been going on. Level with
          us. What happened in there?

                    RAY
          All right, you want the truth? Zombies
          were trying to steal some paintings for
          some reason. I think this all ties
          into the rioting and the local
          robberies. Somebody needs a large sum
          of money, very quickly. I think they
          need it to buy bullets to build up a
          bigger zombie army.

                    SGT. ACKERMAN
          You should have stuck with your first
          well crafted piece of bulls...

                    SGT. RODRIGUEZ
          Ackerman, go call HQ. I'll call the
          lieutenant and fill him in.

Ackerman shrugs his shoulders and heads back to the police
car.

                    RAY
          You believe me?

                    SGT. RODRIGUEZ
          Look, Ray. We all know what's going
          on. I also know you're a good guy.
          Shoot, my father was once saved from a
          were-bear by a luchadore. I know
          you're the real deal. I'll talk to the
          lieutenant. Until things settle down
          I'm going to see if we can at least
          stop pestering you.

                    RAY
          You mean I'm not going to get hassled
          every time someone with a mask robs a
          bank?

                    SGT. RODRIGUEZ
          No promises. I can try though. We'll
          go over the surveillance tapes at the
          hangar. If your story checks out, you
          might have saved all our lives. We
          stick by our own.

                    RAY
          That's great, Sgt. Rodriguez. If you
          don't mind, I'd like to see that tape,
          too. There was something about that
          zombie general that was odd.

                    SGT. RODRIGUEZ
          You mean other than him being dead and
          all?

                    RAY
          I've got some friends that might find
          any information useful.

EXT. AIRPLANE HANGAR -- DAY

Marlil and Lycaeon emerge from their hiding place and look
quizzically at Ray.

                    LYCAEON
          The boys in blue didn't take you
          downtown?

                    RAY
          No. It would appear I'm no longer a
          usual suspect. They are going to go
          examine the surveillance tape further.
          This may finally be the break I've been
          looking for.

                    LYCAEON
          Break? You're really getting into
          this.

                    RAY
          I'm starting to feel like a real
          professional. Thanks to you guys, I
          don't know what I would have done
          without you.

                    MARLIL
          We've only begun upon the path. There
          will be many more pitfalls before this
          is journey is complete.

                    LYCAEON
          Thanks, oh great teacher. Dude, just
          tell the kid not to get cocky.

                    RAY
          How about we just look and see what the
          police brought me and go from there.

Ray pulls out a picture the police gave him. It is a
digital image of Glendalton taken from the surveillance
tape.

                    LYCAEON
          He is one ugly, mother f...

                    MARLIL
          Glendalton Frigardson, a true monster.
          Amalgamated from the slain bodies of a
          thousand soldiers. He was supposed to
          be a great hero for his creator.

                    LYCAEON
          Instead he turned into this
          schizophrenic monster that destroyed
          the geek who made him and went
          ballistic.

                    RAY
          Very Frankenstien's monster. I get it.
          He didn't really seem the psychopath to
          me. He was almost honorable.

                    LYCAEON
          He's a bit more Adam than monster.
          Glendalton has a bit too much of
          everything. The kid from MIT that made
          him got all the DNA he could from old
          battlefields.

                    RAY
          MIT? Wait a second, this all sounds
          like some old cartoon show I saw once.
          Didn't that happen on GI Joe?

                    MARLIL
          Once again the reference is lost to me.
          The creator wanted him to be a great
          warrior, instead he also had pacifist
          blood in his veins. He is constantly
          conflicted.

                    RAY
          Which makes him more dangerous than I
          realized. I watched some of the video
          with the cops. I thought he had a weak
          guard on his left. He was trying to
          sucker me into hitting his left. He
          would have clocked me.

                    MARLIL
          I told you he was amalgamated from
          thousands of soldiers. He will be a
          formidable opponent.

                    RAY
          He didn't strike me as the evil genius
          type though. He said something about
          his mistress.

                    MARLIL
          The zombie queen. I believe you may be
          right about them looking to raise funds
          for some sort of army of the damned.

                    RAY
          It's the only thing that makes sense.
          A large army needs a lot of weapons. A
          lot of weapons cost a lot of money.

The police cars start racing off in the distance. Sirens
blaring. Ray rushes back toward them.

EXT. AIRPLANE HANGAR -- DAY

Ray races up to the police cars as the last ones are
pulling out. He runs up to Officer Rodriguez.

                    RAY
          Come on tell me what's the rush?

                    SGT. ACKERMAN
          You saved all our lives in there, Ray.
          I owe you one.

                    SGT. RODRIGUEZ
          Some big hairy things are attacking a
          car dealership across town. Sounds
          like the officers could use a
          luchadore.

                         RAY
          You offering me a lift?

                         SGT. RODRIGUEZ
          No can do. Don't you have a car?

                         RAY
          Can't get a license since I wear the
          mask.

                         SGT. ACKERMAN
          We'll have to see about that.

                         RAY
          I have another way. I'll see you
          there.

The police get in their car and take off. Marlil and
Lycaeon race forward.

                         LYCAEON
          Well? What's the word.

                         RAY
          A car dealership under attack by
          monsters. Think we can port?

                         MARLIL
          I have not the strength.

                         LYCAEON
          Neither do I. Besides we'd need to see
          it to safely make it there.

                         RAY
          Then we've got a big problem. I think,
          though, I might have a solution.

                         LYCAEON
          You're going to get us there?

                         RAY
          You bet.

EXT. CAR DEALERSHIP -- DAY

Police cars surround the area, the dealership looks like a
bomb hit it. Cars are smashed to pieces. A yellow cab

pulls up and Ray gets out of it, followed quickly by
Lycaeon and Marlil. Lycaeon pays the driver.

                    LYCAEON
          Sorry about the radio... and the cd
          player. I hope that'll cover it.

Lycaeon races over to Ray and Marlil. Marlil looks winded
and rests heavily on his staff.

                    RAY
          Are you all right, Marlil?

                    MARLIL
          I have not used this much energy in
          over a hundred years. I believe my age
          is catching up to me.

                    LYCAEON
          I agree. I think you're getting too
          old for this shit.

                    RAY
          Just sit tight, Marlil. We'll make you
          proud on this one.

                    LYCAEON
          I think I should sit this one out as
          well. Big hairy monsters aren't really
          a specialty.

                    RAY
          Are you afraid?

                    LYCAEON
          Hell yes. I'm not sure this is my
          thing. I don't want to end up food for
          some giant hairy thing.

                    RAY
          We don't even know what we're up
          against.

INT. CAR DEALERSHIP -- NIGHT

Large hairy WERE-WOLVES are tearing apart the dealership.
They are not looking for something specific but appear to
be simply causing carnage and destruction. The wolves walk
on long legs with large wolf-like features. Full snouts

with large teeth and long claws make the classic modern
movie were-wolf. They are swarming over the dealership.

One large wolf with a white stripe down its back stands
tall above the others. He pulls a car door off its hinges
and hurls it into another vehicle.

EXT. CAR DEALERSHIP -- NIGHT

Ray is introducing Lycaeon and Marlil to the police.

                    RAY
          These guys are helping me. I know its
          asking a lot, but they need to be
          allowed the same access I have.

                    SGT. ACKERMAN
          If I didn't know any better I'd say
          they were freaking were-wolves in
          there.

                    SGT. RODRIGUEZ
          You don't know any better and they
          probably are. When a luchadore is on
          the case, you know something strange is
          going on.

                    RAY
          What happened to Bureau 13? Didn't
          they take care of this sort of thing.

                    SGT. ACKERMAN
          I don't know what the hell you're
          talking about.

                    SGT. RODRIGUEZ
          Yeah, what are you talking about?

                    RAY
          A group of folks that took care of this
          sort of thing. I thought they were
          government funded.

                    SGT. RODRIGUEZ
          Nothing I ever heard of. Then again, I
          never really saw most of this crazy
          shit. Christ, since SWAT got taken out
          in the riots the other day, we've been

just trying to maintain what little
order we can.

                    LYCAEON
So anybody got any silver bullets?

                    SGT. ACKERMAN
Are you kidding?

                    LYCAEON
Actually I am. I do need silver though,
just hoping for the most obvious
choice.

                    MARLIL
These officers do not need your levity,
Lycaeon. They do need our assistance.
What they must accomplish is to supply
us with any silver trinkets they can
supply us with.

                    SGT. ACKERMAN
Is he for real?

                    RAY
Yes he is. So you got any silver? I
know better than to doubt these guys.

                    SGT. RODRIGUEZ
I'll see what we can come up with.

The officers leave the cover of the police car to begin
their search.

                    RAY
So are you guys going to magic up some
silver bullets?

                    LYCAEON
It's not that easy. Are we doing an
infusion, Marlil?

                    MARLIL
It is a fair assumption you make. Ray,
we intend to assemble as much silver as
we can. We will then infuse its very
essence into you.

                    LYCAEON
Whoa. I figured we'd just infuse it
into the guns of the cops. That's a
lot of fur flying in there.

                    MARLIL
That is why I will not risk the lives
of these officers.

                    LYCAEON
But you're willing to waste our silver
by infusing it into a person and not a
weapon. What's he supposed to use
silver fists?

                    MARLIL
Precisely. He will defeat many foes.
Bullets can only defeat one per round
fired.

                    LYCAEON
I guess you've got a little more trust
in the man than I do.

                    RAY
I'm right here, guys. Don't talk about
me like I'm invisible.

                    LYCAEON
That spell wore off. The nice thing
about this infusion is it should last
for a few days. If all goes well and
you survive that is.

                    RAY
I think I can handle were-wolves.

                    LYCAEON
I'm talking about the spell. Humans
aren't really supposed to be infused
with metal. I've never tried it
before.

                    RAY
Great.

INT. COMTESSE CAMPANELLA'S CHAMBER -- NIGHT

Comtesse Campanella has Glendalton tied to a mystic altar.
The room is a black and white apartment filled with all
manner of unusual artifacts and fine art. A large altar
with strange carvings of snake-like creatures dominates the
room.

                    COMTESSE
          So you just happened to lose that
          shipment?

                    GLENDALTON
          Not at all, mistress. The police were
          reinforced.

                    COMTESSE
          How? There is no one able to reinforce
          them.

                    GLENDALTON
          There were many men, mistress. They
          had magical weapons. They were well
          trained. You know I would not fail you
          otherwise.

                    COMTESSE
          As you have said. I just find it
          unusual that considering all our raids,
          two that you have overseen were
          failures.

                    GLENDALTON
          Mistress, you know I can not stand the
          pain of failing you. You have my word
          as a soldier.

                    COMTESSE
          That's not what I want. I want your
          utter devotion. I did not create you.
          I will however enjoy destroying you.

                    GLENDALTON
          Mistress, you know I live to serve you.

                    COMTESSE
          Most men die to serve me.

The Comtesse weaves her hands and magical energy pours forth which racks Glendalton with pain.

EXT. CAR DEALERSHIP -- NIGHT

                    SGT. ACKERMAN
          This is all we could get. I hope it's
          enough.

Ackerman dumps a bag of rings, pendants, and other trinkets on the ground.

                    MARLIL
          This is more than adequate. Ray,
          prepare yourself.

                    RAY
          Um... How should I do that?

                    LYCAEON
          Flex your shoulders.

Ray flexes and follows the next few instructions for a moment.

                    LYCAEON (CONT'D)
          Good. Now roll your head. Loosen up a
          little. Swing your arms in a wide
          circle. Now the most important part.
          Stand with your legs apart. Put your
          head between your legs and kiss your
          ass goodbye.

                    RAY
          Very funny.

                    LYCAEON
          The scary thing was, I really thought
          you were going to do it.

                    MARLIL
          Enough! Ray, place your hands above
          the silver items.

                    LYCAEON
          Here goes nothing.

                    LYCAEON AND MARLIL TOGETHER
          CALAH METALA! KABKAGAG BUR MAK!

The silver items dissolve into a cloud of energy and it
floats up. The energy coats Ray's hands and causes him to
sparkle slightly.

                    RAY
          Uh, guys, this is a little strange. I
          feel very weird.

The energy cloud sparkles until there is a flash of thunder
and lightning. Ray's hands glitter with energy the rest of
his body is surrounded by a glittering aura for a few
moments.

                    LYCAEON
          What do you know? He lived. Man, I'm
          better than I thought.

                    MARLIL
          We are better than you thought.
          Although I do believe we did more than
          make his fists silver. The infusion
          has turned his entire body into a
          silvered aura.

                    RAY
          Well I always tell my students to use
          your whole body as a weapon. I guess I
          get the chance to show it.

                    SGT. ACKERMAN
          That was some light show. We lost
          three guys in there. You sure you
          don't want backup?

                    RAY
          Keep your men back. I've got work to
          do.

Ray runs straight into the car dealership and launches
himself at the first were-wolf he sees.

INT. CAR DEALERSHIP -- NIGHT

Ray crashes through the entrance of the dealership and into
the first were-wolf. He plows into beast. His punches and
kicks cause the were-wolf to cry with rage. A quick head
chop behind the back of the wolf's head causes it to
crumple to the ground.

Ray quickly turns and launches himself at a pair of were-
wolves approaching him. He wraps his legs around one wolf
and his arms around the other. He chokes them both to
death with the limb locks. He quickly flips up onto his
feet and turns to the lead striped wolf and another wolf
beside him.

The ALPHA WOLF has a large stripe on his back. The Alpha
leaps into the air to land on Ray like a tiger on its prey.
Ray sidesteps the massive lunge and strikes a blow on its
massive back. The beast howls with rage. Ray quickly
spins and prepares for the second wolf.

The second wolf strides over a car and leaps at Ray. The
luchadore briskly side steps and pounds a chop into its
large back. The Alpha wolf has regained its footing and
bites at Ray. It's teeth break off on the silver infused
luchadore. Ray laughs.

The wolves whimper and whine since the Alpha has been de-
fanged. Ray stands proudly.

                    RAY
          Get out of my city, you toothless curs,
          or I'll make rugs out of the rest of
          you.

The wolves slink away into the shadows. Ray grabs the
Alpha.

                    RAY (CONT'D)
          Not so fast, stripe. I'll want words
          with you after you change back.

                    ALPHA WOLF
          That will not be necessary. I can
          speak.

                    RAY
          Well that's useful! So what's going
          down?

                    ALPHA WOLF
          I have no idea of what you speak.

                    RAY
          Zombies attacking shopping malls,
          vampires looting warehouses, and now

were-wolves trashing a car dealership.
I get the feeling you know more than
you are telling me.

          ALPHA WOLF
We have a list of acceptable targets.
We attack or rob them. Then we get
rewards.

          RAY
What sort of rewards?

          ALPHA WOLF
Larger claims of hunting land, totems
of power, and more.

          RAY
So who's paying you?

          ALPHA WOLF
Couldn't say. It is just posted on our
pack web site.

          RAY
Web site?

          ALPHA WOLF
It's the easiest way to keep up with
all members of the pack.

          RAY
All right, give me the address and any
passwords needed.

EXT. CAR DEALERSHIP -- NIGHT

Ray steps out of the dealership. The cops look relieved to
see him. Marlil and Lycaeon also seem very relieved.

          MARLIL
Where are the wolves?

          RAY
Gone and not coming back. I took out
their Alpha. They won't be bothering
anyone again.

          SGT. ACKERMAN
You let them go?

                    LYCAEON
          Not smart, Ray. They'll be back
          preying on innocents as soon as
          possible.

                    RAY
          He surrendered, according to the code
          of luchadores I can not harm him
          further.

JOHN PROUDFEATHER the Native American owner of the car
dealership pulls up in a very nice car. He wears a nice
suit with a large native American medicine necklace. He is
quite distraught.

                    SGT. ACKERMAN
          Hi there, John. We couldn't stop all
          the damage, but it was minimized to the
          main showroom.

                    JOHN PROUDFEATHER
          When I came in earlier I honestly
          didn't expect anything to be standing.
          You guys did one hell of a job.

                    SGT. RODRIGUEZ
          We didn't do anything. We owe it all
          to Ray here.

                    JOHN PROUDFEATHER
          Ray? And just who are you, masked man?

                    RAY
          I'm Ray. These two here are Marlil and
          Lycaeon. They are my advisors. We
          tried to get here as fast as we could.

                    SGT. RODRIGUEZ
          Yeah, we work with these folks as
          advisors in areas out of our usual
          field. The handle our most unorthodox
          cases. Sadly since they aren't
          official they can't ride with us.

                    JOHN PROUDFEATHER
          This town's not that big. I'm sure
          they got here as fast as they could.

                    LYCAEON
         Well, getting a cab was pretty tough
         due to all the riots and such.

                    JOHN PROUDFEATHER
         A cab? You take on Loup Garou and ride
         in a cab?

                    MARLIL
         You know of the Garou?

                    JOHN PROUDFEATHER
         My father was the medicine man of our
         tribe. I know all about that sort of
         thing.

                    RAY
         I'm so sorry we couldn't get here
         sooner to save the rest of the stock.

                    JOHN PROUDFEATHER
         Well we simply can't have a hero of the
         people traveling in squalor. With the
         amount of money you saved me, I think I
         can arrange something.

                    LYCAEON
         Hell yeah! We're getting some wheels!
         Can we make sure it has a roomy back
         seat?

EXT. ANTON DAVORIK'S CORPORATE HEADQUARTERS -- EVENING

Anton Davorik is livid. He stares intently at his monitor.

                    ANTON DAVORIK
         We're not making our quota. We're at
         least three percent below goal. What
         the hell is going on?

Rupert Maltheon walks up to his desk from his computer
area.

                    RUPERT MALTHEON
         It's the local operations. Someone has
         stopped three local incidents. Do you
         think the vamps failed when they took
         out the Bureau team?

                    ANTON DAVORIK
          I doubt it. Everyone of that team have
          been accounted for in the larder area.
          Except for Amanda Winters of course.
          Philip of Macedonia wanted her for his
          new bride. He assures me he's taming
          her quite well.

                    RUPERT MALTHEON
          So it's got to be some other white hat?
          The Wizard's High Council?

                    ANTON DAVORIK
          Unlikely. By the time those old fools
          decided to interfere we'll be done and
          ruling the underworld and this one.

                    RUPERT MALTHEON
          So who do you think?

                    ANTON DAVORIK
          I intend to find out. Pull four oracles
          from the stock market division. It's
          going to bottom out soon from our
          operation anyway. Let's see what the
          sisters divine about our foe.

                    RUPERT MALTHEON
          Any other personnel transfers?

                    ANTON DAVORIK
          Let's get the Comtesse to bring a
          brigade close by. If it is a new
          player on the block, I'd like to get
          some intelligence on him.

INT. RAY'S NEW CAR -- NIGHT

Ray pulls up in the convertible car of his dreams. Lycaeon
rides shotgun and Marlil sits in the middle rear. They
pull up and park behind Ray's Apartment building.

                    RAY
          Well we didn't really need the Mp3
          player anyway.

                    LYCAEON
Sorry, but I love that song. I got
excited.

                    RAY
Note to self: if I get any other tech
stuff, don't let Lycaeon get excited
around it.

                    LYCAEON
Oh, you're no fun.

                    RAY
I maybe no fun, but I got wheels and a
license.

                    MARLIL
You are really coming into your own,
Ray.

                    LYCAEON
I wonder how long that silvering will
last.

                    MARLIL
It should wither after the moon begins
to wane.

                    LYCAEON
You could just say, "in a few days."

                    MARLIL
I believe that was the meaning I
conveyed.

                    RAY
Do I have to separate you two? It's
like having a couple of four year-old
kids in the car.

                    MARLIL
I apologize, Lycaeon. I am merely
weary.

                    LYCAEON
It's ok, old-timer. I'm beat, too.

                    RAY
          Then let's get some rest. I have a
          feeling we've got an even bigger day
          tomorrow.

INT. RAY'S CHILDHOOD HOME LIVING ROOM -- NIGHT

BEGIN DREAM SEQUENCE

Ray enters his childhood home and sees his parents lying in
a pool of blood. He looks over at the table and sees a
luchadore mask and a note from his parents. In a haze he
grabs the mask and puts it on. Then he heads out to battle
dozen zombies burst through the door at him.

INT. RAY'S APARTMENT -- DAY

Ray jolts awake. He looks at his nightstand and sees more
chili-dog wrappers.

                    RAY
          Why do I do this to myself?

Lycaeon stirs in his sleep.

                    LYCAEON
          No more wire hangers.

INT. OUTSIDE OF THE GYM -- DAY

Military grade zombies are surrounding the gym and they
have some of the folks hostage including Maroni.

                    GLENDALTON
          Tell me the name of the masked warrior
          and no harm shall come to you.

                    MARONI
          I don't know his full name. He just
          goes by Ray. I have to pay him in cash.
          He never takes the freaking mask off.

                    GLENDALTON
          Where do you pay him?

                    MARONI
          At the venues. I'm not even sure where
          he lives.

                    GLENDALTON
          I find that unlikely. How do you
          contact him?

                    MARONI
          I've got his phone numbers. His home
          number and his work number.

                    GLENDALTON
          Phone numbers? That will prove most
          helpful.

INT. RAY'S APARTMENT -- DAY

Ray and Lycaeon are flipping channels. There are reports
of zombie attacks all around. There is no attempt to
discredit the zombie stories now. People are panicking.

                    RAY
          Looks like we've got some work to do.

                    LYCAEON
          Too bad the Wizard's Council doesn't
          pay overtime.

                    MARLIL
          Tempus Fugit, gentlemen.

                    RAY
          What does that mean?

                    LYCAEON
          It's Latin for, "it's time to kick butt
          and take names."

INT. ANTON DAVORIK'S OFFICE -- DAY

Rupert and Anton are going over Glendalton's report.

                    RUPERT MALTHEON
          You've got to hand it to the big
          Frankenstein. He's placed your boy in
          less than 3 hours. I still haven't
          found him on any of the extra-
          dimensional nets.

                    ANTON DAVORIK
          I told you he is not some grand
          champion from an alternate dimension.

I don't even think he's a true
luchadore. He's just someone who
wishes he was a super-hero. What else
have you found with the information
from Glendalton.

                    RUPERT MALTHEON
Well, actually plain old Google was
pretty handy in this case.

                    ANTON DAVORIK
I don't care how you got the
information. Just give me everything
you've got.

                    RUPERT MALTHEON
His name is Ray. He wrestles for
charity. Other than that it's almost
like he doesn't exist. No driver's
license, no social security card, no
credit cards, no last name, not even a
boy scout membership. He's not in any
professional wrestling league. Shoot I
can't even find a video membership or
My Space page. Glendalton lucked out
getting his agent. That guy pays him
in cash, since he apparently never
cashes checks.

                    ANTON DAVORIK
So what do you think?

                    RUPERT MALTHEON
I think the guy is covert ops. Nobody
has records that clean. I think he's
Shop.

                    ANTON DAVORIK
He's definitely not Bureau 13. We've
interrogated the rest of the local
group.

                    RUPERT MALTHEON
Since he doesn't have a license, I've
got Glendalton spreading his troops
around the town. He can't be far. I
figure our man, Ray, will poke his mask

out when we hit close enough to home
and we can tail him to his lair.

                ANTON DAVORIK
Glendalton was able to get us the
number of a community outreach program
for youngsters where the fool helps the
less fortunate. He's got a soft spot
for kids in trouble. Send some Alpha
wolves to hunt the children in the
area.

                RUPERT MALTHEON
Didn't you read the last report? The
Alpha Wolves are MIA. I told you they
couldn't be trusted to stick to any
sort of plan.

                ANTON DAVORIK
I find that hard to believe. It must
have been our friend Ray. He probably
believes himself to be a true champion
of good. He might even believe himself
to be a true luchadore. This is all
very much their modus operandi. I've
just never heard of one operating here
in the states. Let alone so close to
here.

The Comtesse Campanella walks into the room. She strolls
right up to Anton's desk.

                COMTESSE
I know of one luchadore that once
worked in America. It wasn't that long
ago. A lone warrior stopped a whole
battalion of my minions in a small town
not too far from this very place.

                ANTON DAVORIK
Rupert, focus you attentions on that
town. If you can't find anything than
Comtesse you have my permission to raze
the town.

                COMTESSE
I've been dying to replenish my forces.
That town has been a thorn in my side

for too long. Will it affect your
other operations if I pull a brigade
away?

                    ANTON DAVORIK
          Not at all. I've got another man on
          the job that should give me just the
          windfall I need to meet Gun's price and
          then some.

EXT. VIDEO PAVILION -- DAY

Video Pavilion is one of those chain video stores.
Zombie's are swarming the place. Ray pulls up with Lycaeon
and Marlil in the car.

                    LYCAEON
          Looks like a party for the new Romero
          release.

                    RAY
          Either that or Marilyn Manson has a new
          CD out today.

                    LYCAEON
          Funny. There's hope for you yet.

                    MARLIL
          The references are lost on me. I
          assume that hey have something to do
          with zombies in popular culture.

                    RAY
          Now you're getting it.

                    MARLIL
          Your silvering seems to still be in
          effect. That should prove most
          efficacious.

                    LYCAEON
          Amazing return to form there, Marlil.
          You could just tell him that you've
          still got silver magic in you. Go kick
          some butt.

                    RAY
          Silver works on zombies?

                          LYCAEON
            Not really any better than anything
            else, but it makes your skin as hard as
            silver so punching them in the head
            will make their brains go squish much
            easier.

                          RAY
            I see.

Ray leaps out of the car and onto a pile of zombies. He
then proceeds to wade into the group. Lycaeon turns to
talk to Marlil while Ray battles the hordes of the undead
in the background.

                          LYCAEON
            So when are you going to tell him
            you're dying?

                          MARLIL
            How long have you known?

                          LYCAEON
            I'm a fucking wizard remember? I was
            also your own damn apprentice. Don't
            pretend like you didn't think I'd
            noticed.

Ray grabs a zombie and pulls him down across his knee in a
back-breaker move. He then throws the lifeless husk to the
ground.

                          MARLIL
            All wizards have their time. We are
            not immortal, just long lived. Your
            time will come as well.

                          LYCAEON
            Yeah, but I'll still be better looking
            than you.

                          MARLIL
            I am going to pay no mind to that last
            flippancy. Have you come up with a
            gift for our young friend?

Ray climbs up on a post in front of the store and elbow
drops onto a zombie, crushing its head in the process.

                    LYCAEON
          I'm still not sure he's who I should be
          giving anything. I've yet to see him
          do anything truly heroic.

                    MARLIL
          Has he not done many wondrous deeds of
          valor and courage?

                    LYCAEON
          Oh don't get me wrong. The kid can
          fight. I just think if he's getting an
          Excalibur, he better be worthy of it.
          I don't need a Lancelot, I need an
          Arthur.

Ray grabs a zombie by its feet and begins to swing it in a
circle like a helicopter blade, knocking down many more
zombies.

                    MARLIL
          We all have our failings, my former
          apprentice. I think Ray would make a
          fine hero.

                    LYCAEON
          Well let's see about getting you fixed
          up after this, too. I know this
          alchemist on Waters Avenue that makes
          dandy potions.

                    MARLIL
          An alchemist? I thought most of them
          were in Europe.

                    LYCAEON
          They are, but this guy's a local. He
          set me up with some love potions...
          for... for a friend. A sad and lonely
          friend of mine needed some potions.

                    MARLIL
          I see. Perhaps the alchemist can
          assist Ray since you seem reluctant.

                    LYCAEON
          Was that a snide comment? I'll help
          the kid when I'm good and ready. It

                    may not be a gift, but that doesn't
                    mean I won't watch his back.

Lycaeon points a finger at a zombie that's about to grab
Ray from behind and blasts it with a laser like beam of
energy. It bursts into flames and falls behind Ray. Ray
keeps on fighting, oblivious to the near fatal attack.

EXT. RECREATION CENTER PLAYGROUND -- DAY

More military zombies are scouring the playground area for
clues. One finds a framed copy of the newspaper article on
the wall of the center. The headline is "Masked Hero Saves
Kids." He grabs it and staggers over to Glendalton.

                         GLENDALTON
                    Thank you, sergeant. We have our man.
                    It's him.

Glendalton speaks to his earpiece.

                         GLENDALTON (CONT'D)
                    We have our target acquired. It is as
                    you expected it to be.

                         ANTON DAVORIK (V.O.)
                    Good. Send the men to grab all the
                    children in the area.

                         GLENDALTON
                    Home invasions, sir?

                         ANTON DAVORIK (V.O.)
                    You heard me. Grab them and bring them
                    to a central area. We'll flush him
                    out.

                         GLENDALTON
                    Respectfully, sir. Killing children in
                    battle is strictly against the articles
                    of war.

                         ANTON DAVORIK (V.O.)
                    You foolish thing, you should read some
                    of the modern day villains handbooks.
                    They use children as weapons in Jihad.
                    Children are acceptable losses if

victory is achieved. Surely you know
about Hiroshima and Nagasaki.

                    GLENDALTON
          Sir, I will do as ordered, but under
          formal protest.

                    ANTON DAVORIK (V.O.)
          Duly noted, soldier.

Glendalton signals his zombies to spread out in a search
and capture operation.

INT. ANTON DAVORIK'S OFFICE -- MOMENTS LATER

Anton is pulling off his earpiece.

                    ANTON DAVORIK
          I'm think I'm starting to figure out
          how to deal with that guy. It's a good
          thing my father was a military man.

                    RUPERT MALTHEON
          He was?

                    ANTON DAVORIK
          I felt very sorry when I had to slit
          his and mother's throats to seal my
          deal with Satan. I was quite
          remorseful for almost a whole day.

                    RUPERT MALTHEON
          That when you started getting promoted?

                    ANTON DAVORIK
          Of course. Satan kept his part of the
          bargain, I was head of the company
          within a month. I wonder if I'll see
          my father when I rule Hell?

                    RUPERT MALTHEON
          I just want a shot at Marilyn Monroe
          and Mae West.

                    ANTON DAVORIK
          Really? I will have command of all the
          hordes of the underworld, and you
          simply want a piece of undead tail?

                    RUPERT MALTHEON
          I've got a thing for blondes with
          big... talent. So sue me.

EXT. RECREATION CENTER PLAYGROUND -- MOMENTS LATER

Ray and the wizards are driving by the schoolyard when they
see the zombies dragging, Richard, the young ruffian out of
a house.

                    RAY
          They've got, Richard. That's too going
          too far.

Ray pulls the car in front of the zombies and leaps onto
the first one. Marlil creates a dagger of flame in mid air
and it hurls itself at the other zombie. Ray twists the
head off the other zombie and quickly covers the eyes of
Richard.

                    LYCAEON
          Nice job with the dagger. You never
          taught me that one.

                    MARLIL
          I've got to keep some things secret.
          Isn't that what a wise old wizard is
          supposed to do.

                    LYCAEON
          Very cute. How's the kid, Ray?

                    RAY
          A little shaken up, but he seems ok.

                    RICHARD
          They wanted to know where you lived. I
          didn't know. Then they wanted to know
          if I knew where any of the other kids
          lived. I shouldn't have told them, but
          they were going to hurt, Mom and Dad.

                    RAY
          It's ok, Richard. Where are your
          parents?

                    MIKE
          They're inside. They knocked them out
          with darts from their guns. The big
          monster zombie said, not to kill anyone
          that didn't fight back.

                    RAY
          It's got to be that guy from the
          airport. This is odd though. It just
          doesn't seem like he would have done
          this.

                    MARLIL
          I will go and aid this young man's
          parents. You should go seek the other
          children and stop this before anyone
          else is endangered.

Marlil walks out of the room to find Richard's parents.

                    RAY
          Richard, which kids did you tell them
          about?

                    RICHARD
          All of them. I'm sorry.

                    RAY
          They would have invaded every home in
          the area to get that information. You
          saved a lot of innocent lives today.

                    RICHARD
          Then how come I feel horrible?

                    RAY
          Dont' worry, you did the right thing.
          Saving your parents was the right thing
          to do. We'll get a chance to stop them
          now.

Lycaeon walks up.

                    LYCAEON
          Marlil says the kids parents are going
          to be just fine. Let's get going.

                         RAY
              Richard, stay with your parents until
              they wake up. They'll be fine and so
              will you. Don't worry about the other
              kids. I'm on the case.

EXT. SMALL HOUSE -- DAY

BEGIN MONTAGE

Ray and Lycaeon pull up and defeat another couple of
zombies. Rescuing a SMALL CHILD (Age 5-8) around the same
age as Mike.

EXT. ANOTHER SMALL HOUSE -- DAY

Ray punches through another zombie rescuing another CHILD
(Age 5-8).

EXT. FAST FOOD RESTAURANT -- DAY

Lycaeon casts a whirlwind to stagger the zombies while Ray
frees THREE CHILDREN (Age 10-14) from them. Ray turns and
attacks them.

INT. CHILDREN'S PLAYROOM -- DAY

TWO KIDS (Age 10-14) are playing video games on their TV
when zombies smash through the window behind them. The
kids scream and run for cover. Ray and Lycaeon burst in
right behind them. Lycaeon freezes one with a blast from
his rod, while Ray smashes the other one into a wall.

INT. ALLEY -- DAY

Zombies stalk a YOUNG BOY (Age 4-6) and Sally into the
alley. Glendalton steps up behind them and grabs them.

END MONTAGE

EXT. AIRPLANE HANGAR -- DAY

Ray, Marlil and Lycaeon pull up to the hangar from before.

                         LYCAEON
              What makes you so sure he's bringing
              them here?

                    RAY
          Elementary, my dear Lycaeon. He's
          trying to find me by grabbing the kids.
          He doesn't really want them, he wants
          me. This is the only place I've seen
          him. He knows that, too. This is
          where he'll be.

                    MARLIL
          The military jeep parked in front of it
          is also a dead giveaway.

Lycaeon and Ray turn in disbelief to the old wizard.

                    LYCAEON
          Did you just make a quip?

                    MARLIL
          No. I merely stated the obvious as you
          two seem to always enjoy.

                    RAY
          You've taken your first steps into a
          larger world.

                    MARLIL
          Your reference is lost to me...

                    RAY AND LYCAEON TOGETHER
          But you understand its meaning.

                    LYCAEON
          So very predictable, Marlil.

Ray steps out of the car.

                    RAY
          You guys got any ideas?

                    LYCAEON
          Don't get shot or eaten.

                    MARLIL
          Try to distract them long enough for
          Lycaeon and I to transport the children
          out of harm's way.

                    RAY
          No problem. I'm going to give up.

                    LYCAEON
What?

                    RAY
You heard me. I can not allow any
innocent to be harmed by action or
inaction.

                    LYCAEON
If they take you out, then no one will
stop them.

                    RAY
Then get those kids to safety and I'll
get free.

                    MARLIL
That will be accomplished without
delay.

                    LYCAEON
He means, "No problem." Go for it,
Ray.

INT. AIRPLANE HANGAR -- DAY

Ray walks into the hangar right through the main door.
Glendalton has a few KIDS (varied ages 6-15) tied up next
to the back of the hangar.

                    RAY
I'm not here to fight you.

                    GLENDALTON
That's good, I-am-not-a-wizard.
Because you would lose.

                    RAY
I know that. I know you were trying to
sucker me in that last fight. I hope
you also know that I can not allow any
harm to come to those children.

                    GLENDALTON
That is good, because I do not wish to
harm them any further. My master
simply wants you.

                    RAY
You don't seem like the master
following type. I figured you as a
general.

                    GLENDALTON
I was many things, soldiers, medics,
even a field cook. I was a knight. I
was a footman. I was a king. I have
so many memories of both sides of many
battles.

                    RAY
And what do those memories tell you
about this battle.

                    GLENDALTON
That I am on the wrong side. However,
the mistress controls all dead flesh,
and sadly I am her puppet in this
matter.

                    RAY
I'd like to help you if I can.

                    GLENDALTON
I wish you could. The Comtesse is not
one to be trifled with.

                    RAY
Neither am I.

                    GLENDALTON
I do not wish to harm these children.
These tactics are deplorable.

                    RAY
Then let them go.

                    GLENDALTON
I can not. You can defeat me. If you
do so, the children will be released.
If you fail, the children will still be
released as we will have no further
need of them.

                    RAY
          Then it looks like you and I have to
          throw down.

                    GLENDALTON
          I just want you to know one thing.

                    RAY
          And that is.

                    GLENDALTON
          There will be no world for these
          children if you lose. You must defeat
          me. I could not bear to continue on in
          the world my master intends to create.

                    RAY
          Who controls you then, a Master or your
          Mistress?

                    GLENDALTON
          As I am a slave to my Mistress, she
          hungers for the power of my master.
          They will rule the world, unless
          stopped.

                    RAY
          How can I stop them?

                    GLENDALTON
          By stopping me.

Glendalton quickly draws his gun and fires several
controlled bursts from his machine gun at Ray. Ray dives
for cover and tries to sneak along behind some of the
crates.

                    GLENDALTON (CONT'D)
          Come now, Luchadore. One of the pieces
          of myself was once rescued by the great
          El Santo himself. Surely you will not
          be a coward and tarnish the code of
          Luchadore!

                    RAY
          My code is to save those children no
          matter the cost. I'm merely observing
          you to learn your tactics.

                    GLENDALTON
        Or you're waiting for me to run out of
        ammo.

                    RAY
        That, too.

                    GLENDALTON
        I know you, Luchadore. You have to
        defeat me, but you don't know how.

                    RAY
        I think I do.

Ray leaps from behind a crate and knocks the gun from
Glendalton's hand. They slam into the side of the plane
still parked in the hangar. Glendalton pulls a knife from
his boot and stabs Ray, but the blade bounces off
harmlessly.

                    GLENDALTON
        Silvered skin? That was not expected.

                    RAY
        I had to take some dogs for a walk.

                    GLENDALTON
        You defeated the alphas?

Glendalton flips Ray over his back and lands him in a
sleeper hold. Ray begins to gasp. He struggles to speak.

                    RAY
        Somebody had too.

                    GLENDALTON
        Don't fight it, just go to sleep. The
        children will be unharmed. They will
        find peace for a day or two.

Ray uses all his strength to lift Glendalton off the ground
and flips him over into a pile-driver.

                    RAY
        They will find peace and happiness as
        long as there is a breath in my body.

Ray rolls to his feet and grabs Glendalton's knife from
before. He holds it to the fallen zombie soldier's throat.

                    RAY (CONT'D)
Now let those children go.

                    GLENDALTON
You forget yourself, Luchadore. I know
you won't kill me.

                    RAY
That's where you're wrong. You're
already dead.

                    GLENDALTON
Then you have learned the secret.

                    RAY
That you're a zombie? That's no
secret.

                    GLENDALTON
No. That I have no life worth living
anymore.

                    RAY
Then help me stop this impending doom.
Join the good guys.

                    GLENDALTON
A noble king once offered me mercy
once. I gladly took it. Then another
part of me killed that very king on the
same battlefield. I can not ever hope
to redeem myself of all those acts.

                    RAY
Those acts weren't who you are. They
are pieces of someone else's past.
Just find who you are.

                    GLENDALTON
I am Glendalton Frigardson.
Amalgamation of warriors of old and
new. I was created to defeat the
bullies of my creator at his school.

                    RAY
You even have a name.

                    GLENDALTON
          It was the only name found on any of
          the bodies he used to create me.

                    RAY
          It is a good strong name.

                    GLENDALTON
          Aye it was.

                    RAY
          It still is.

                    GLENDALTON
          I have clans to honor. Horrors of war
          to atone for. Unjust battles and
          cowardly acts of unfit soldiers.

                    RAY
          No you don't. You have yourself and
          the innocents you can help save. That
          is the code of the luchadore. One does
          not right the wrongs of the past. One
          fights for the good of today.

                    GLENDALTON
          Lower the blade. I yield.

     Lycaeon steps forward.

                    LYCAEON
          Besides, Marlil and I got the kids out
          about three minutes ago.

                    GLENDALTON
          Wizard I know thee.

                    LYCAEON
          I wouldn't be surprised. I've been
          around a bit.

                    GLENDALTON
          You swindled some sailors of their
          spending cash in Vietnam not too long
          ago.

                    LYCAEON
          I might have done that.

                    GLENDALTON
Without that money, they were forced to
spend the night in a hovel.

                    LYCAEON
Well they shouldn't have gambled money
they couldn't afford to lose.

                    GLENDALTON
True. They had to learn to live off
the kindness of another for days. It
changed one of them forever.

                    LYCAEON
I hope for the better.

                    GLENDALTON
Yes. For that harsh lesson I will tell
you of the fate of the world in a mere
one day's time.

                    MARLIL
Speak, noble warrior. Tell us and I
can ease the pain in your mind.

                    GLENDALTON
The Master intends to damn the last
true soul. He will then be crowned the
new Prince of Darkness.

                    MARLIL
The last true soul?

                    GLENDALTON
He knows it's location. He knows the
true soul's weakness. He also has his
Gun.

                    MARLIL
Tell me more.

                    GLENDALTON
I fear I cannot while the Mistress
still has my flesh at her command. She
has placed many blocks in my brain.

                    MARLIL
          Rest well, Glendalton. It will not be
          long before you may rest truly.

                    LYCAEON
          You did good, Frankenstein. Real good.

                    RAY
          I take it we just got a major clue.

                    MARLIL
          One that will take cunning to decipher.

                    RAY
          Glendalton Frigardson, it was an honor
          to meet you in battle. You should
          return to your mistress before you are
          missed.

                    GLENDALTON
          That I will. I will be punished for
          failing her again. If I survive that
          experience I will send you any
          information I can.

                    RAY
          Just go away. Run to safety.

                    GLENDALTON
          That is impossible. I do not fear
          death. I have felt it many times
          before. I only hope I can fight at
          your side instead of against you
          sometime.

                    RAY
          It would be an even greater honor.

INT. SMALL HOUSE -- DAY

Ray, Lycaeon and Marlil are talking to some of the kids.
The kids are working on a computer with Sally.

                    RAY
          You're sure about this, Richard?

                    SALLY
          Yes. All the attacks are avoiding
          business run by Davorik Conglomerated.

                    LYCAEON
I really need to find a way to use the
internet. It would save me a fortune
in crystal balls.

                    RAY
You just want it for all the porn.

                    LYCAEON
Perish the thought.

                    MARLIL
I do not understand this line of
inquiry.

                    RAY
I'm following the money. Someone is
financing all these attacks. They have
all been for money or insurance claims.
It's almost as if he's daring someone
to notice that he's clean.

                    LYCAEON
Either that or he thinks he's
invincible.

                    RAY
So how do we stop him?

                    LYCAEON
Can't they just "Google" it?

                    RAY
It doesn't work that way.

                    SALLY
Actually it does. Davorik
Conglomerated has their corporate
headquarters downtown.

                    MARLIL
Lycaeon, I think it's time we visited
that alchemist friend of yours. My
magic is fading fast from exertion.

                    LYCAEON
          Good point. I also think Ray's
          silvering is starting to fade. He's
          lost that healthy glow it gave him.

                    RAY
          Alchemist?

                    LYCAEON
          We're going to get you some magic
          potions to go kick the bad guy's butt.

INT. ANTON DAVORIK'S OFFICE -- DAY

Anton's hands clench his desk in frustration as he rises
from his chair.

                    ANTON DAVORIK
          What did you say?

                    COMTESSE
          Glendalton's brigade failed us,
          dearest.

                    ANTON DAVORIK
          Why did you not handle that operation
          personally?

                    COMTESSE
          I found something much more useful for
          you.

                    ANTON DAVORIK
          We had him in our grasp. What could
          possibly be more useful?

                    COMTESSE
          I found a small church. They send him
          money and supplies so that he might
          continue his frivolous crusade.

                    ANTON DAVORIK
          He is subsidized by the church? I
          didn't expect a Vatican agent to be
          active in North America, that will make
          Gun's task all the more difficult.

                    COMTESSE
          Not at all, he is not from the Vatican.
          It is a small church that is doing this
          out of gratitude for his rescuing them
          years ago.

                    ANTON DAVORIK
          So how is this better than having him
          in my grasp?

                    COMTESSE
          Because, I have the address where they
          send the money. Plus I have her.

The Comtesse points over to a newly installed caged area in
the office. Inside are a dozen or so people including
FATHER RODRIGO and Carlotta. The Comtesse indicates
Carlotta by pointing directly at her.

                    ANTON DAVORIK
          And who is she?

                    COMTESSE
          I believe her to be our mysterious
          hero's lover. She has pictures of him
          throughout her room. She even had
          this.

She pulls out of her bag a scrapbook with a large heart on
the cover. It is filled with articles about Ray and the
good deeds he has done.

                    ANTON DAVORIK
          Excellent. Move her from the cell into
          something a bit more comfortable. I
          wouldn't want our prize damaged.

                    COMTESSE
          You are pleased?

                    ANTON DAVORIK
          Just deal with that failure of a
          general you've got. We're too close
          now to Gun's deadline. I can't afford
          to have anyone not performing at one
          hundred and ten percent at this point.

                    COMTESSE
          I've got just the thing to tear
          Glendalton's soul apart.

EXT. VIDICARE'S APOTHECARY -- DAY

Vidicare's Apothecary has a small store front and the
windows are filled with jars and ointments. The stores
around it are in disarray, but it appears to have avoided
all the zombie carnage.

Ray, Lycaeon and Marlil enter the shop.

INT. VIDICARE'S APOTHECARY -- DAY

The shop is clean and filled with tons of unique jars
filled with strange colored liquids

A small bell sounds when Marlil and Lycaeon enter. Ray
steps in behind them.

MARQUIS DE VIDICARE steps out into the room from an office
area behind the counter. He is very handsome and appears
very affluent. Not at all what someone would expect a
alchemist to look like. He looks more like he belongs in
corporate America.

                    MARQUIS DE VIDICARE
          My dear Lycaeon, don't tell me you need
          another supply of Tribal Passion
          already?

                    LYCAEON
          Ixnay on the ovelay Otionpay. I'm here
          to seek potions for my colleagues.
          We're going to need potions of energy,
          potions of vitality, some sort of
          potion of invulnerability, and a potion
          of intense lust to distract our
          enemies.

                    MARLIL
          I find it quite telling that you only
          described the reason for the last
          potion.

MARQUIS DE VIDICARE
As do I. These potions would not be
difficult as you know. Payment from
you however is always difficult.

MARLIL
I can assure you we are able to pay his
debts and any costs for these potions.

MARQUIS DE VIDICARE
Assurances I don't need. Money I don't
need. Ingredients I do need. I'll need
four ounces of wizard's blood from the
two of you and three hairs from the
hero.

MARLIL
I've never heard of such nonsense. No
wizard would ever dare give that kind
of power to a stranger.

LYCAEON
In the jar as usual, Vidicare?

MARLIL
You've given him your essence before?

LYCAEON
No. I've only given him blood. I've
never given him my essence. I have
trouble when it comes to filling cups.

MARLIL
That's what I meant, fool. You've
given him more than he needs. Wizard's
blood would be far too powerful in the
wrong hands.

MARQUIS DE VIDICARE
If the price is too steep, then I
suggest you vacate my shop. I already
have a pretty tall order in place.

MARLIL
Are you the same Marquis De Vidicare
that was court magician to Elizabeth
the First?

                    MARQUIS DE VIDICARE
That I am, wizard. You have heard of
me?

                    MARLIL
Considering Shakespeare based a
character on your exploits, I think it
was hard not to have heard of you.

                    MARQUIS DE VIDICARE
Travesty and parody, that hack could
not capture my true essence.

                    RAY
Which character?

                    MARLIL
Prospero, fellow wizards had to go into
hiding for several years thanks to this
man's rather public actions. The
Inquisition was started by more of your
actions if I recall.

                    MARQUIS DE VIDICARE
All that is ancient history. All I do
now is perfect my studies and make a
modest living selling my services to
those in need.

                    LYCAEON
Well as you can see we are in need.

                    MARQUIS DE VIDICARE
I merely have to ask one thing. Why
the sudden need for all this?

                    RAY
Haven't you been watching the news, or
looked out your storefront? The world
is in chaos, zombies and were-wolves
are stalking the streets in broad
daylight. The world is going to hell
in a hand-basket.

                    MARQUIS DE VIDICARE
Your point being?

                    RAY
          We need those potions to help stop it.

                    MARQUIS DE VIDICARE
          Oh, I'm afraid I can't allow that.

                    MARLIL
          And why is that false wizard?

                    MARQUIS DE VIDICARE
          I just received a proper contract to
          turn several hundred tons of lead into
          gold for a client, and he's assured me
          a proper place in the new world order.
          I'm afraid you three might put a
          wrinkle in that plan.

The Marquis grabs a vial off the wall and throws it at
Marlil. The wizard raises his hand to create a mystical
barrier but some of the potion splashes onto him. He falls
screaming to the ground.

Ray bounds over the counter at the Marquis who quickly
drinks down a blue potion from a vial. Vidicare's eyes
begin to glow with a red flame. His smile broadens as large
fangs grow forth. It is an impossibly huge smile of fangs.
He begins chomping at Ray.

Lycaeon races over to his fallen mentor.

                    LYCAEON
          Marlil! What can I do?

                    MARLIL
          Stop him from killing our last hope. I
          will be fine in a few moments. The
          potions effects are not fatal.

Ray and Vidicare are fighting viciously and knocking over
rack after rack of potions. Strange combinations of
magical energies are filling the room from the smashed
bottles. The wind picks up from a broken jar of a tornado
potion. Two potions smash together and create an army of
small knights that charge after a small dragon released
from another jar.

Lycaeon scours the shelves to find something useful.

Vidicare forces Ray to the ground and opens his huge mouth.
The teeth are even longer than before and it looks like he
could swallow Ray's head in one bite.

Ray frees a hand and reaches for a potion on the counter.
He smashes it onto the head of the Marquis. The Marquis
falls back screaming.

Ray looks at the potion. The label says, "Bat Urine, great
for removing stains and purging evil spirits."

                    RAY
          That was handy.

                    LYCAEON
          Ray, he'll only be weak for a moment or
          two. Use this.

Lycaeon tosses Ray a necklace with a small dagger that pops
out of the end of it.

Ray pops the dagger and plunges it at the Marquis.

Vidicare rolls away and has recovered from the potion's
effects that was smashed on his head. His face is now
twisted and bits of skull are showing through. He bounds
over to Marlil who is still trying to regain his feet.

The Marquis picks him up easily and wraps his now clawed
hands around Marlil's throat.

                    LYCAEON (CONT'D)
          Master!

                    RAY
          No!

                    MARQUIS DE VIDICARE
          Stay back, fools, and I might let him
          live. You've already cost me a great
          deal of time and effort here. It will
          take me years to recreate all those
          potions. Thankfully I will be
          immortal.

                    MARLIL
          Sadly you aren't now.

Marlil summons a bolt of lightning from the still swirling storm in the room. It blasts the old wizard and the Marquis out through the window.

EXT. VIDICARE'S APOTHECARY -- MOMENTS LATER

Marlil and the charred remains of the Marquis land harshly on the ground outside the shop. Ray and Lycaeon rush out to check on their fallen friend.

                    LYCAEON
          You old fool, we could have taken him.

                    MARLIL
          I could not let him take my power or
          essence. He would have become
          unstoppable then.

                    RAY
          How long will it take you to heal?

                    MARLIL
          I will not be healing from that blast.
          It was my own magic that harmed us. A
          wound by my own magic will never heal.

                    LYCAEON
          So I guess you won't be accompanying us
          to the final battle.

                    RAY
          Let's get him to a hospital. We can
          debate that later.

                    MARLIL
          I've had enough of apothecaries and
          science. I think it's simply best if
          you left me in peace. Scour the
          Marquis' shop and see what you can find
          about his employer.

                    RAY
          What do you want to bet it's Davorik
          Conglomerated.

                    MARLIL
          It would be foolish to bet against
          that. Now go. I must be at peace to

disperse my energy back to the world
that brought me forth.

                    LYCAEON
          Till the next life, my friend.

                    MARLIL
          Till the next life, my son.

Ray starts to say something and reach down for Marlil, but
Lycaeon grabs him and leads him away.

                    RAY
          What are you doing? We can help him.

                    LYCAEON
          No, we can't. He's helping us, though.
          He's going to call forth a sunburst
          with the last of his energy.

                    RAY
          What's that?

                    LYCAEON
          It will fill the world with a pure
          source of mystical energy for a few
          moments. It should be enough for all
          the wizards to notice.

                    RAY
          What will that do?

                    LYCAEON
          Hopefully get them off their asses and
          get them to help. If nothing else it
          will severely weaken every vampire and
          other creature of darkness for about a
          100 mile radius.

                    RAY
          How long will it last?

                    LYCAEON
          I don't know. It depends on how much
          energy the old man has left. If we're
          lucky, it might last a whole day.

                    RAY
          Will he survive?

                    LYCAEON
          No.

There is a bright flash of golden light that blinds
everyone and turns the screen white for a moment.

                    RAY
          His sacrifice shall not be in vain.
          Let's find where Davorik was supposed
          to accept delivery of several tons of
          gold.

EXT. COMTESSE CAMPANELLA'S CHAMBER -- DAY

Glendalton is once again strapped down to an altar. The
Comtesse walks around him.

                    COMTESSE
          You are a puzzlement to me. You are
          dead flesh, and yet you resist my
          commands.

                    GLENDALTON
          I do not resist, mistress. I merely
          question the tactics and honor of our
          master.

The Comtesse smacks the amalgamated corpse.

                    COMTESSE
          Insolent fool, he is not my master. He
          is my lover. When he has succeeded in
          ruling hell, I shall destroy him and
          take the throne myself. The dead shall
          rule the world.

                    GLENDALTON
          I will be your general, mistress.

                    COMTESSE
          No, it is too late for that. My dear
          creature, you have too many minds, too
          many souls. To control you completely
          I must destroy them all.

                    GLENDALTON
          No, mistress, my memories are all I am.

                    COMTESSE
          Then I hope you like the new you. In
          fact I'll order you to enjoy your new
          life as my loyal servant when you are
          as mindless as those you command.

The Comtesse raises her hands and begins chanting.
Glendalton screams in agony.

INT. RAY'S APARTMENT -- DAY

The apartment is destroyed and ransacked. The picture of
El Santo has been smashed. Everything Ray holds dear has
been broken into hundreds of pieces.

                    LYCAEON
          Ray, I'm sorry.

                    RAY
          It's not an issue, Lycaeon. These are
          just things. We've lost a friend.

                    LYCAEON
          That may not be the worst of it. If
          they've learned where you live...

                    RAY
          Then they may know who I am. Oh god, I
          didn't even begin to worry about home.

                    LYCAEON
          There's no time for that now. We've
          got to stop Davorik. He needed the
          money by 10 pm tonight. That gives us
          only a few hours to figure out what he
          needs it for.

                    RAY
          Glendalton said something about the
          last true soul. And that his master
          already had his gun.

                    LYCAEON
          Did he say gun? Or did he mean Gun?

                    RAY
          Excuse me? You're starting to sound
          like Marlil.

                    LYCAEON
          I'm sorry. I'm just wondering if he
          meant a gun or the Gun. Gun is hell's
          hitman. He's a contract killer. He's
          got bullets made from thirty pieces of
          silver that you might be familiar with.
          Anyone shot with those is instantly
          damned to hell. No matter how pure
          they are.

                    RAY
          What does that mean?

                    LYCAEON
          Hell puts a hit out on holy rollers
          like presidents, kings and other holy
          men. It isn't to simply assassinate
          someone, they want them to burn for
          eternity.

                    RAY
          Lincoln, Pope Paul?

                    LYCAEON
          Several emperors, Reagan, George
          Reeves, and both Kennedy's. Even if
          they survive the shot, they could be
          tainted and damned.

                    RAY
          So who is the last true soul and how do
          we save him?

                    LYCAEON
          You mentioned the Pope. Isn't he in
          America on his first tour of the
          states.

                    RAY
          They're going after the Pope. It's
          time to call in some favors.

Ray runs over to the phone.

                    LYCAEON
          One second there, Ray. I've got
          something I think you're going to need.

Lycaeon walks over to the table and begins casting a spell.
The mystical energies swirl and sparkle over the table.
The energy forms into a cape and mask. The mask is
strikingly similar to Ray's current mask but now the Aztec
sun on the front has a crown in front of it.

                    LYCAEON (CONT'D)
          I give you, great champion, a mask of
          power and a kick ass cape to go with
          it.

                    RAY
          I don't know what to say.

                    LYCAEON
          Thank me later and put them on. I dub
          thee Rey Supremo, The High King.

Ray pulls off his mask and pus on the new one. Once again
we do not see his see his face. He then pulls on the cape.
He turns.

                    RAY
          Let's ride.

EXT. ANTON DAVORIK'S CORPORATE HEADQUARTERS -- NIGHT

Mercenaries and guards patrol the grounds of Anton's
Headquarters which now looks more like an armed fortress.
Were-wolves replace security dogs. Zombie soldiers are
stationed at key locations. It looks like a fortress of
darkness.

Sirens blare in the distance and the guards and soldiers
turn. A fleet of police cars pull up with Sgt. Rodriguez
and Sgt. Ackerman's car leading the escort for Ray's
convertible. Ray's cape flies in the wind behind him.

The soldiers open fire on the police and cops all scramble
for cover as they pull in to form a barricade line.

                    RAY
          You men, just keep them busy. Lycaeon
          and I will try to get in there and
          stop them at the source.

                    LYCAEON
          We will?

                    RAY
          We have to. The silvering has worn
          off, but I'm dying to see how this
          wonderful mask and cape hold up under
          pressure.

                    LYCAEON
          Let's do this.

The two break from the crowd and charge into battle.
Police fall into formation behind them and try to advance.

Lycaeon raises a mystical barrier to block most of the
incoming fire. Ray reaches the first line of soldiers and
begins to wade into them with fists flying.

All seems to be going well, until a door opens and a horde
of zombies pours out onto the field. The Comtesse is
leading the group of zombies made from the corpses from
Ray's hometown. Included are Ray's Parents and Glendalton.
Ray is stunned when he recognizes some of the zombies.
When he sees his parents he falls to his knees .

                    LYCAEON (CONT'D)
          Get up man, we've got incoming.

                    RAY
          It's my parents, Lycaeon. It's the
          dead from my old town. What do I do?

                    LYCAEON
          Help them rest. Make them proud. Do
          you think they want to be this?
          They're just shells. Your parent's
          souls are fine. Stop them, man.

                    RAY
          Bastards! You will pay for this
          blasphemy!

                    LYCAEON
          Now that sounds like a hero.

Ray and Lycaeon charge into the oncoming horde. But there
are too many of them. Glendalton grabs Lycaeon and pulls
him down under the swarm. Ray, too begins to falter. The
Comtesse laughs.

At that point a series of jeeps pulls up behind the police.
The jeeps are manned by luchadores. They run out of the
jeeps and race forward to engage the zombies. EL HIJO DEL
SANTO pulls Lycaeon free of Glendalton.

                    RAY
          What kept you guys?

                    EL HIJO DEL SANTO
          Marlil's final spell worked for us as
          well. We were able to turn the tide on
          El Satanico. We got here as fast as we
          could after your call. Sadly my
          father's jet is not as fast as we had
          hoped.

                    LYCAEON
          Better late than never.

                    GLENDALTON
          Santo?

                    EL HIJO DEL SANTO
          A zombie that speaks? This is new to
          me.

                    GLENDALTON
          I was once saved by your father. He
          rescued my entire platoon from a mad
          djinni. I remember. I remember
          everything.

                    RAY
          Can you fight her control?

                    GLENDALTON
          I can do better. Soldiers, I order you
          to break off fighting the luchadores
          and the officers. We fight for the
          High King and The Saint. Destroy the
          Comtesse and our former master's
          minions.

                    COMTESSE
          Fool. They will not cross Comtesse
          Campanella, the zombie queen. I
          control all the souls of the dead.

                    GLENDALTON
          No! You control their flesh. Their
          souls are free.

The zombies turn on the Comtesse and tide turns.

Here and there we see shots of luchadores wrestling various
soldier zombies, vampires and were-wolves.

                    LYCAEON
          Ray, they can hold them here. It's
          time we headed inside to stop the
          source of this madness.

                    RAY
          Thank you again, El Santo. It is an
          honor to fight along side you.

                    EL HIJO DEL SANTO
          My the spirits of grace guide you.

Ray and Lycaeon break through the front line of defense and
into the building.

INT. ANTON DAVORIK'S CORPORATE HEADQUARTERS -- NIGHT

A large group of vampires carrying various artifacts and
weapons stand in front of our heroes as they enter the
building. Some are vampires of the former Bureau 13 team.
Lycaeon surveys them.

                    LYCAEON
          This is going to be nasty.

                    RAY
          So are we.

The vampire version of Hawk lunges at Ray with a long
sword.

                    LYCAEON
          That's the Sword of Damaclees. If it
          so much as scratches you, you will
          bleed from its wound forever.

Ray dodges the thrust and punches the vampire in the back
of the head.

                         RAY
                No scratching check.

Two vampires charge in at Lycaeon and Ray. One carries a
baseball bat and one carries a battle ax.

                       LYCAEON
                The Ax of Foe and I think that's Pete
                Rose's cursed Louisville Slugger.

Ray grabs the wrist of the vampire wielding the bat.

                         RAY
                I take it all these items are nasty and
                cursed.

                       LYCAEON
                Yeah. My advice is we should get
                through these guys as fast as possible.
                If even one connects its either bad
                luck for seven years or worse.

                         RAY
                We'll get banned form the hall of fame?

                       LYCAEON
                Watch your back. Clinton's veto pen!

Ray turns in time to push the vampire trying to sneak up on
him with a presidential pen into the vampire with the
baseball bat. They collide and the pen stabs the other
vampire. He instantly turns to dust.

                         RAY
                I take it that would have been worse on
                me.

Lycaeon blasts a vampire with an arc of energy form his
staff. The whirls it to impale another vampire charging
him with a ancient sledge hammer.

                       LYCAEON
                Oh no you did not just try to hit me
                with old John Henry. You are all going
                down.

Ray grapples a trio of vampires that are holding a series
of martial arts style weapons, including nun-chucks, a
katana, and a pair of sais.

                    RAY
          Look! Its the Teenage Mutant Ninja
          Vampires.

                    LYCAEON
          Be careful man, they might not look
          like much, but those weapons make
          Crouching Tiger effects possible in
          real life.

The vampires fly through the air as if in some martial arts
film. The leap and bound effortlessly as they slice at
Ray.

                    RAY
          Great, now I wish I had taken that
          gymnastic class at the YMCA.

Lycaeon blasts one of the trio out of the sky and is
beginning to show signs of tiring. He has spent far too
much energy too fast. A vampire moves to grapple him.

                    RAY (CONT'D)
          You've got one coming up behind you,
          Lycaeon. Blast him.

Lycaeon turns to block the assault with his staff. The
vampire knocks him to the ground and climbs on top of him.
It is Chastity as a vampire.

                    LYCAEON
          I can't. Too much juice too fast.
          Then again, I think she might be used
          to that.

Ray is being held back by the last swarm of vampires. He
can't aid his fallen friend.

                    CHASTITY
          What's the matter, lover boy? Am I
          still too much woman for you?

                    LYCAEON
          It's time for the modern wizard's best
          friend.

                    CHASTITY
          Don't worry, I'll save that part of you
          for last.

Lycaeon flicks his wrist and a .38 special revolver falls
into his hand.

                    LYCAEON
          I'm breaking up with you, Chastity.
          You've gone too goth.

Lycaeon pulls the trigger and slams her into a wall.

He then squeezes off a few more shots at the crowd of
vampires around Ray.

Ray is able to break free of the crowd thanks to the assist
and wastes no time finishing off the last of the vampires.

                    RAY
          Thanks for the assist. I'm sorry about
          Chastity.

                    LYCAEON
          Let's just make this son-of-a-bitch
          pay. I'm tapped out but I'm still
          pretty handy with this staff, and I've
          got another couple of rounds of silver
          bullets in old Betsy here.

                    RAY
          You had silver bullets?

                    LYCAEON
          As a last resort. I knew you could
          handle those were-wolves.

                    RAY
          We've got to have a long talk, soon.

INT. ANTON DAVORIK'S OFFICE -- NIGHT

Ray and Lycaeon blast into the room. They look around and
see Rupert Maltheon at the computer desk burning files onto
disks. Anton Davorik is standing on his desk with a spear
and wearing a suit of ancient armor.

                    ANTON DAVORIK
          Hello, Ray. I've been dying to meet
          you.

                    RAY
          I don't believe we've had the pleasure.

                    ANTON DAVORIK
          I am Anton Davorik. I am about to
          become the new ruler of Hell and then
          the Earth. I've already made my
          payment. You're about ten minutes too
          late to save the world. You are a poor
          luchadore.

                    RAY
          Once I stop you, you won't be ruler of
          anything.

                    ANTON DAVORIK
          I'm wearing the Armor of Alexander. I
          carry the Sword of Alexander, and the
          Spear of Destiny. No one who holds
          these can be defeated.

                    RAY
          Then why doesn't Alexander still have
          them.

                    ANTON DAVORIK
          I also have a bargaining chip.

Anton motions against the wall and shows Ray the caged
area. Three were-wolves sit atop the cage as the people
huddle on the floor of the cage.

                    ANTON DAVORIK (CONT'D)
          I have merely to give the word and my
          puppies shall eat those who support
          you.

                    RAY
          You know I won't allow that to happen.

                    ANTON DAVORIK
          Also, I've got her.

Anton motions to the upstairs area where Carlotta is tied
to an altar. Several DARK ROBED CULTISTS surround her.

                    ANTON DAVORIK (CONT'D)
          Your girlfriend up there dies if you do
          not stand down and call off the other
          luchadores.

                    RAY
          You know as a luchadore, I can not tell
          a lie.

                    ANTON DAVORIK
          So.

                    RAY
          I don't even know her name.

                    ANTON DAVORIK
          You must be lying. She had a scrapbook
          about you. She had written letters of
          love to you.

                    RAY
          I can not lie. I tell you again, she
          is not my lover. I do not even know
          her name.

                    ANTON DAVORIK
          Oh well, the blood of a virgin will aid
          my friends up there anyway. It really
          matters little. If you defeat me, I
          still win.

                    RAY
          How's that?

                    ANTON DAVORIK
          The last soul is doomed to damnation.
          Even if I die, the plan is in motion.
          I will rule the underworld in a matter
          of minutes.

                    RAY
          Then I guess we've got to cut this
          short.

                    LYCAEON
          Got the doggies, Ray. You sick the
          dude in the dress. We'll meet at the
          cultists.

Lycaeon draws his gun and opens up on the were-wolves that
leap from the cage to charge him. Ray jumps at Anton.

Anton swings the spear at Ray and it bounces harmlessly off
Ray's Cloak.

                    ANTON DAVORIK
          Impossible!

                    RAY
          Excalibur couldn't pierce that cloak.
          What makes you think some old spear
          can.

Anton throws the spear at Ray who dodges it effortlessly.
He then draws his sword.

                    ANTON DAVORIK
          Speaking of Excalibur, lets test that
          theory of yours.

Ray and Anton clash in a fight that rages throughout the
room. Anton thrusts at Ray who dodges the blow. Ray flips
over Anton. Ray pulls a string on the back of the armor
loosing it. Then Ray climbs up the ladder toward the
library section. He leaps off it onto Anton. The evil
corporate mastermind in armor slashes violently at the
flying luchadore. Ray lands a strong hammer punch on
Anton's chest as he lands.

Lycaeon meanwhile is fighting off the were-wolves with the
few bullets he has left. He fires two shots into one
approaching wolf, downing it. He backs into Rupert's
computer bank which begins to catch fire and smokes from
the wizard's touch.

                    RUPERT MALTHEON
          My porn! My beautiful hard drives of
          extra-dimensional porn! Die, you
          bastard!

Rupert reaches for Lycaeon who ducks just as a were-wolf
leaps at his head. The lycanthrope slams into Rupert which
rips off his head.

                    LYCAEON
          Bad dog, no biscuit.

Lycaeon summons a little energy which is all he currently
has and energy lances from the end of his staff to
incinerate the were-wolf.

Then he starts climbing the ladder to the cultists.

Anton slashes Ray with the sword and blood flows from his
chest.

                    ANTON DAVORIK
          So you're not invincible.

                    RAY
          Neither are you.

Ray pushes Anton and he staggers back onto the Spear he
threw earlier. He cries out as it pokes through his chest.

                    ANTON DAVORIK
          I may die but I've already won.

                    LYCAEON
          That's where you're wrong, buddy.

Lycaeon is holding Carlotta and is surrounded by
unconscious cultists. His staff is bent slightly form all
the heads he has knocked.

                    CARLOTTA
          Ray! You have to save him!

                    LYCAEON
          Man, I can't win. Ray saves my girl
          and she goes to him. I save his girl
          and she still goes to him.

                    CARLOTTA
          He already paid the gunman to kill the
          priest.

                    LYCAEON
          The priest? Not the pope?

                    CARLOTTA
He was talking to the Pope. Anton
already had him in his pocket. The
priest in the front of the car is the
target.

                    RAY
Thank you. I'm sorry. I don't even
know your name.

                    CARLOTTA
I'm Carlotta Alonzo. You saved me when
we were children.

                    RAY
I know. I've dreamt about you ever
since.

                    CARLOTTA
So have I.

                    LYCAEON
We don't have time for this. I need
juice and I need a TV.

                    CARLOTTA
Why?

                    LYCAEON
I've got to get your boyfriend there to
the Pope's vicinity to save the priest.
I only hope one of the news channels
has got it covered.

                    CHRISTINE (ON INTERCOM)
Mr. Davorik, the live feed you've
requested will be on your screen in
moments.

                    LYCAEON
That'll do. Boy, I hope she's a sexy
as she sounds.

                    RAY
Can you get me there?

                    LYCAEON
          Sure. There's enough juice in all
          these artifacts to get you to the moon
          if I had to. It's a one way trip
          though. I'll fry the monitor.

                    RAY
          It's ok. You stay here in case any
          other wolves, vamps or who knows what
          tries to hurt these people.

                    LYCAEON
          You've got it. We've got signal. Look
          for a man with a black cowboy hat. I
          hear Gun likes the theatrics.

                    RAY
          Will do.

                    LYCAEON
          Be careful.

                    RAY
          You bet.

Carlotta runs up and kisses him. Ray smiles. Lycaeon
begins the spell.

                    CARLOTTA
          For luck.

                    LYCAEON
          Have you got any luck for me? Or maybe
          a sister?

EXT. PLAZA -- NIGHT

Ray appears in the middle of a crowded plaza. Huge throngs
of people are trying to get close to the Pope in the
Popemobile. A YOUNG PRIEST with an innocent face sits in
the front, non-armored section of the car.

Ray has only seconds to move and fight his way through the
crowd. He sees Gun heading toward the Popemobile.

With only seconds to spare Ray launches himself like a
missile to take the bullet for the young priest just as Gun
draws and fires.

Ray is slammed back against the popemobile.

The crowd panics and Gun curses and tries to slink away.

                    GUN
          DAMN NATION!

Ray staggers to his feet and the crowd backs away.

                    RAY
          Hey, Gun! Don't you want your silver
          back?

Ray pulls the bullet off his mask which protected him.

                    GUN
          How in the hell did you do that?

                    RAY
          I am Rey Supremo. I am luchadore.

Gun draws his gun and prepares to fire.

Ray jumps up on the hood of the Popemobile and runs across
the crowd to tackle Gun. He gets him in a hammerlock. Gun
tries to turn his gun on Ray but drops it. It goes off as
Gun staggers back.

He looks at the blood coming from his chest.

                    GUN
          Well I guess I was damned anyway.

The young priest rushes up to give last rites to the dying
gunman.

                    RAY
          You know he was about to kill you. Not
          the Pope.

                    PRIEST
          He is still one of god's creatures. It
          is only right he should find peace and
          absolution.

Ray begins to speak but then reporters surround him.

EXT. MOVIE THEATER PREMIER -- NIGHT

A large crowd surrounds a movie theater several
superimposed headlines and magazine covers flash in front
of the screen.

"MASKED HERO SAVES POPE!"

"AMERICA ADORES LUCHADORE"

"LUCHA, LIBERTY AND THE PURSUIT OF JUSTICE" a comic book
featuring Rey Supremo.

"AMERICA'S GREATEST MAGICIAN WOWS PRESIDENT" an article
with Lycaeon at the White House

"DEPARTMENT OF HOMELAND LUCHADORE FORMED" "Rey Supremo
appointed as head."

"Bureau 13? How Government Spending May Have Cost Us."

After the headlines fade we see the title of the movie is
"Rey Supremo Versus the Gun of the Damned." Dozens of
reporters and hundreds of fans are snapping pictures as Ray
and Carlotta pull up to the red carpet in his convertible.

                    REPORTER NUMBER ONE
          Rey Supremo, is it true you're going to
          retire from the N.W.E. undefeated.

                    RAY
          It's only fair to let others wear the
          belt.

                    REPORTER NUMBER TWO
          When's the wedding date?

                    CARLOTTA
          We still haven't decided, but soon.

                    REPORTER NUMBER ONE
          Is it true you helped pick the new Pope
          after the recent scandals that rocked
          the Vatican?

                    RAY
          I can not confirm or deny that. I can
          say that the new Pope is a good man and
          has a true soul.

                    REPORTER NUMBER THREE
                 (IN SPANISH)
          Is it true you're going to be visiting
          Mexico for the baptism of the grandson
          of El Santo?

                    RAY
                 (IN SPANISH)
          Wild horses couldn't keep me away.

They begin to make their way down the carpet when Ray's
phone begins to beep.

                    EL HIJO DEL SANTO (ON PHONE)
          Rey, fishermen off the Pacific Coast
          have spotted a large creature making
          its way from an island near Japan
          toward the coast.

                    RAY
          I'm on it. Traffic will be a pain, but
          I'll make other arrangements.

                    EL HIJO DEL SANTO (ON PHONE)
          Call me if you need any assistance.

                    RAY
          I can handle it. Besides I've already
          got back-up.

Ray pushes a button and dials another number.

                    RAY (CONT'D)
          Christine, it looks like I'll need a
          lift to the coast.

                    CHRISTINE (ON PHONE)
          Of course, sir. Supremo One has
          already been dispatched.

                    RAY
          Better get your boyfriend on the way,
          too. I think this one might be big.

                    CHRISTINE (ON PHONE)
          He's already on his way.

A moment passes and a ladder drops from above. The crowd
looks up to see a helicopter with Rey Supremo's logo on the

side of it. As Rey heads for the ladder, Carlotta rushes
up to kiss him.

                    RAY
          Enjoy the film. I'll be back before
          the big finish.

                    CARLOTTA
          You had better be. Otherwise the kids
          will miss getting your autograph.

                    RAY
          We can't have that.

Ray climbs up the ladder as the helicopter heads off for
the coast. A moment latter a flying surfboard with Lycaeon
on top flies close to Ray.

                    LYCAEON
          You didn't think I'd ride some broom
          like that kid did you?

The pair laugh as the fly toward the sunset. A large
shadow rises against it.

FADE OUT

www.ingramcontent.com/pod-product-compliance
Lightning Source LLC
Chambersburg PA
CBHW052144170626
46812CB00004B/1580